THE WINSHIP AFFAIR

A Carrie Bloomfield Novel

by

Phillip E. Temples

Blue Mustang Press
Boston, Massachusetts

Cover image: © Vince Clements/Shutterstock.com

ISBN: 978-1-935199-18-2
PUBLISHED BY BLUE MUSTANG PRESS
www.bluemustangpress.com
Boston, Massachusetts

Printed in the United States of America

For my best friend and life-partner,
Barb Ariel Cohen, Ph.D.

PROLOGUE—AUGUST 1974

"Carrie, wake up!"

The 4-H leader shook the teenage girl out of a sound sleep.

"Mmmmmmmmmmmmm…"

She looked up at the woman, smiled, and asked, "What's wrong?"

"Nothing. But there's something you need to see. All of you: put your things on and come with me!"

A moment later, Carrie, accompanied by eight other girls, trekked down the barn loft stairs. In the dim moonlight they made their way past the farm animals and over to the barn door. It was the girls' second night at the Wisconsin State Fair. The strong fragrance of the fresh hay seemed to be bringing a few out of their dazed stupors. They had come from cities and towns across the state to exhibit their science projects. Carrie's project described the effects of light intensity on photosynthetic rates in plants.

As they made their way to a nearby barn, about a dozen boys who were bunking in an adjacent barn joined the girls at the entrance. Already, a small crowd of teenagers had gathered inside. The object of their attention was a birthing cow whose calf was beginning to crown. Several of the girls and boys were looking away from the cow. They were noticeably uncomfortable. A few were giggling nervously. Two boys were jostling and playfully shoving one another.

One girl turned and remarked to the girl next to her, "Gross!" A young lad hollered, "Yechhh!" He made a gesture with his hands as though he was vomiting. His friend snickered.

Finally, the calf emerged completely from the cow. The calf hit the ground; it made a loud "Plop!" sound.

But the event did not repel all of the boys and girls. A few of them could be heard asking questions, "Is he okay?" "Can I touch it?" "Is it a boy or a girl?"

After a few minutes, the kids' questions ceased, their laughter grew less, and their numbers dwindled. The boys and girls returned to their respective barns to catch a few more hours of shuteye for today was the big day—their science projects would be on display to the general public.

But one child still stood there. The 4-H leader put her hand on the shoulder of the girl who was the last remaining witness to the morning's miracle.

"Are you okay, Carrie?"

She nodded.

Together, they observed cow and calf for a few more minutes. Finally, the 4-H leader patted the young girl on the head, and left.

The girl stood silently in front of the cow and her calf for another half hour, mesmerized.

CHAPTER ONE—PRESENT DAY

Carrie got up out of bed and walked into the bathroom. She yawned, and then she examined the naked figure staring back at her in the mirror on the front of the medicine cabinet: tall, slim, athletic build, with short-cropped, sandy hair. There wasn't a single grey hair to be seen. The body wasn't that of a beauty queen, to be sure. But it wasn't unattractive, either. *Handsome* would be the most apt word to describe her.

Not bad for an old lady.

Just last week, someone remarked to Carrie that she didn't look a day over forty and that she found Carrie to be attractive. Carrie wasn't sure if it had been a frivolous compliment, or if the woman had meant more by it. Carrie was used to men—and sometimes, women—coming on to her. At fifty-three years of age, Carrie could see the beginnings of crow's feet forming around her eyes, along with a few other lines on her neck, thighs, and lower abdomen that hadn't been present a few years earlier. But, all in all, she wasn't that unhappy with how she was aging. There was certainly no evidence of flab anywhere on her body. It wasn't surprising, since Carrie walked or biked almost everywhere. *Who needs a car when you live in Cambridge?*

Carrie was still very much enamored of the elaborate, full frontal tattoo that adorned her chest, abdomen, and upper arms. The artwork had now become an integral part of her since receiving the gift over ten years ago. And while the jury was still out on the tiny diamond stud nose piercing, even *that* was beginning to curry favor with her. Carrie thought that it complemented her artwork.

After another brief moment of self-reflection, Carrie showered, dressed, and went into the kitchen to pour herself a bowl of cereal and a cup of coffee. After consuming half a cup of java she felt a little more inspired to face the day. She then grabbed her smart phone and fired up the personal assistant app to check her daily schedule.

"Selma, tell me today's appointments, please."

"Certainly," intoned the mechanical female voice. "You have an eight a.m. appointment entitled 'research' at the Whitehead Institute."

Yep. I have to check on the microfluidics and update my lab notebook with the results of that latest DNA experiment. Oh, and I need to top off the liquid nitrogen tank while I'm there.

Selma continued: "You have a ten a.m. appointment with Howard Stein at the MIT Media Lab."

Hmm…new user interface for the bioinformatics program.

Selma droned on, reminding Carrie about the eleven thirty a.m. lunch at Sebastian's Café with Kathy Eisen in the Kresge Building at the Harvard School of Public Health. After that, she had a one p.m. meeting with Eugene Anderson at Dana Farber Cancer Institute to discuss a joint collaboration on a promising tumor cell diagnostic she was working on in collaboration with Massachusetts General Hospital. Carrie would swing by the Alexandria Lighthouse Life Sciences Incubator in Watertown to attend a lab meeting at three p.m., and then spend a half hour with a post-doc she was mentoring. If time permitted, Carrie would finish her rounds with a quick stop at the lab bench at the Broad Institute in Kendall Square to begin a new experiment.

No rest for the wicked.

A quick check of overnight email, voice mail and SMS texts, and then she was out the door for her first appointment.

Carrie Bloomfield, Ph.D., President, Founder, and Chief Scientific Officer of the virtual company known as Nexus Technologies, launched herself into a typical day—heading in five directions.

* * *

"I don't know how you do it," remarked her good friend and colleague, Kathy Eisen. Dr. Eisen was a Professor of Statistics at the Harvard School of Public Health and the Associate Director for the Center for Biostatistics in AIDS Research. Additionally, Eisen was one of over two dozen worldwide associates who comprised the ranks of Nexus Technologies.

Kathy wolfed down half of a tuna wrap sandwich she and Carrie had agreed to share.

"I mean, come on, you're always on the move, you maintain a presence at…how many sites now? Six? Seven?"

"It's nine, actually," replied Carrie. "But who's counting? I know, I know. I should put down roots like every other entrepreneur. Rent space and establish my own lab. Consolidate. Save time and money. Et cetera, et cetera."

Carrie took a bite from her half of the sandwich. She waved with her free hand as if to dismiss the statement she had just made. A small chunk of tuna fell from the end of her sandwich, landing on the cellophane wrapper. Unfazed, Carrie continued.

"You realize, of course, if I did that—if I established my own lab—it wouldn't be fun anymore. I'd stay there all the time and I'd lose out on the cross-pollination that goes on in this town. It may seem like a lot of trouble to you—popping in and out of the various labs and startups around Boston and Cambridge—but it's key. It allows me to be competitive and stay on top of my game. It's how I know what's hot, how to connect the dots, ask the relevant questions. Explore problems from an outsider's perspective."

She paused for a second to chew.

"I can't begin to tell you the number of times that some new principal investigator has said to me—either out loud or by the look on his or her face: 'This isn't even your area of expertise. How would *you* possibly know?' Well, it's actually *they* who are at a disadvantage by being part of a rigid, established system. They've got their blinders on. They can't see the forest for the trees."

As Carrie spoke, her fingers unconsciously played with the lanyard she wore like a necklace. Nearly a dozen ID cards hung from it. Many of the major research organizations and independent labs in town were represented in the collection. Most were Harvard or M.I.T. affiliated. A few of the badges contained the names of for-profit startups headquartered in the low-rent section of East Cambridge. Carrie referred to the area as the "biotech ghetto." It consisted primarily of shabby one- and two-story buildings lining Bent and Rogers Streets.

Carrie didn't pay leases for any physical space at her hangouts. In fact, she hardly ever had to pay for equipment time and use. Her reputation as a genius for problem solving and collaboration had long ago earned her space gratis at many of these places. Portions of lab benches and office desks throughout the city were marked with simple, handwritten signs that read, "Carrie's bench" or "Nexus." Many a post-doc or junior researcher had standing instructions from his or her principal investigator: "When Dr. Bloomfield is visiting, move your stuff out of the way and assist her with whatever she needs."

Kathy said, "Hey, if it works for you, who am I to argue?"

A moment passed. They both ate without speaking.

Finally, Kathy asked, "So, speaking of pollination, how's your love life these days?"

Carrie grinned and shrugged. "Who has time for a love life?"

Kathy leaned forward, "True. But, you know what they say about 'All work and no play...'"

"Kathy, my work *is* my play. It's where I get challenged and find satisfaction – much more reliably than in a relationship."

"Just make an effort, okay? Men can be fun too."

"We'll see," replied Carrie. "But, in the meantime..." Desperate to change the subject, Carrie reached down into her backpack and dug out a stack of paperwork. "Here's the latest data from that antibody work at the Brigham. I *have* to know if we're at statistical significance yet. Can you crunch some numbers for me ASAP? Pretty please?"

* * *

The day went by at breakneck speed. After leaving the Alexandria Lighthouse Incubator, Carrie took a quick break and stopped her bike just inside the entrance to the Mount Auburn Cemetery.

Constructed in the early 19th century, Mount Auburn Cemetery had ushered in the beginning of the American public parks and gardens movement. In addition to its historic burial plots and novel markers, the 170 acres of grounds held over 5,500 trees. Thousands of shrubs and herbaceous plants dotted its woodlands, hills, and clearings. Carrie liked to stop by whenever she was in the vicinity, if only to clear her head for a few minutes.

Carrie dismounted from her bike. Then she closed her eyes and stood still, drinking in the sounds of the wind and the birds. After a moment, she took a deep breath and then she slowly exhaled. She repeated the deep breathing and exhaling for a couple of minutes. Only then did Carrie check her email and voice messages.

A man she had dated a few times had called earlier wanting to know if he could come over that evening, but Carrie wasn't feeling especially sociable. Perhaps the feelings Kathy stirred up during their lunch conversation troubled Carrie more than she realized.

Indeed, most of Carrie's relationships *had* ended on a sour note. Her first love affair had been with another student her own age while attending Harvard Medical School to earn her Ph.D. Jim was also a doctoral candidate working in the same lab. The relationship was wildly romantic at first, but it began to sour when Carrie realized that Jim was only using her as a means to an end.

The man didn't have a scientific bone in his body!

Jim was a clever manipulator. Before she broke it off, Carrie had been duped into designing a large portion of Jim's first year's experiments as well as interpreting the results for him. If the lab hadn't employed a dishwasher, Jim would no doubt have had Carrie hand washing all of his test tubes and beakers, too.

Her thesis advisor drew Carrie aside one day and asked some not-so-subtle questions as to the nature of her contributions to Jim's work. She was ashamed and humiliated. Probably even more so than Jim, who was faced with the daunting challenge of starting over with another thesis topic. Two months later, Jim withdrew from the Ph.D. program altogether. Carrie heard that he moved out to the West Coast where he became a sales rep for a large pharmaceutical supply house.

Although they were the same age, Carrie had been inexperienced in the lovemaking department. The sting from the recollection of her intellectual "rape" was offset somewhat by memories of the wonderful times they shared together in the bedroom of his small apartment in Boston's Jamaica Plain neighborhood. Still, the whole sordid affair made Carrie determined never to let anyone take advantage of her again.

CHAPTER TWO

Under the cover of a dark, moonless night, two men wearing dark motorcycle rain gear and tight-fitting gloves walked onto a small, dilapidated wooden pier at Sea Farms Marsh, in the peaceful New England town of Falmouth, Massachusetts. They were carrying a heavy burden: each man had a firm purchase on a third man between him. Their captive was bound, gagged and blindfolded. They dragged the helpless man along, his struggles hardly being a match against his much larger captors.

"Here?" asked one of the captors.

"Yeah. This is the place." The first man possessed a strong New York accent. The second man's voice betrayed no regional accent whatsoever. He could have hailed from Chicago or even Pittsburgh. Neither voice betrayed any emotion.

They stopped, and forced their captive down on his knees and into a squatting position. His face was mere inches from the water's surface. The man who first spoke looked at the other; he shrugged his shoulders as if to ask, "Now?" The second man gave a small nod. The first seized the captive man's head and smacked it down hard, chin-first, against the edge of the wooden dock. The impact from the blow made a loud cracking sound. The man issued a muffled groan. Blood gushed from the laceration on his chin. Then they both grabbed the man and forced his head under the water. He struggled and even tried to scream, to no avail. In less than two minutes the victim ceased putting forth any resistance. His struggling stopped; he was lifeless.

When it was over, the two men hoisted the body back up onto the pier, unbound it and removed the gag and blindfold.

"Oops," said the second man.

"Rest in peace, professor," said the first man. They tossed the body back into the water. It drifted away some ten feet before coming to a stop.

"Go get the stuff. I'll prepare here."

A few minutes later, the second man returned with a container filled with items: small nets constructed with fine mesh; collection vessels that looked like ordinary canning jars; a laboratory notebook; and several containers filled with chemicals. The first man picked up a pen, opened the notebook and thumbed halfway through to the first blank page. At the top of the page, he wrote the current date, and the location: *Sea Farms Marsh, Falmouth, MA*—nothing else. Then he casually flipped the notebook into the water near the floating body. The other items they left lying in a neat pile on the dock.

"It pays to be careful, professor," said one of the men. "Otherwise, you might slip and drown."

CHAPTER THREE

Carrie dismounted, and walked her bike down the busy Hampshire Street sidewalk in Cambridge's Inman Square, carefully avoiding passers-by. It was around 4:00 p.m. on a Tuesday afternoon, and already the light was beginning to drain from the late November sky. The recent change from daylight savings time had robbed Carrie and everyone else of even more precious daylight from the shortened day. It made her feel—*blah*. It was, she supposed, another of life's harsh realities.

Wouldn't it be nice if I lived along the equator?

Carrie looked up and noticed the old African American man on the corner ahead of her. She had known Harry for years. He had been working that street corner, and others in Cambridge and Boston, for as long as she could remember, hawking the homeless newspaper *Spare Change*.

Harry interacted with the pedestrians in a unique, almost comedic style. He enjoyed hamming it up for the passers-by. His motions included friendly pleading while dancing a half-jig type of movement. He was an excellent student of human nature and he knew how to motivate people to elicit a reaction.

"What about you, young man? Young LAY-DEE!" He turned this way and that, maintaining eye contact with his potential customers. While most of the people continued by him without making a purchase, it was rare for Harry to not prompt some sort of response: a smile here, or a "hello" there, or some faint nod of recognition. Harry was definitely *not* an anonymous face, nor did he fit the mold of the unseen, homeless person.

"*Spare Change* newspaper! Help the homeless."

Harry looked over at Carrie as she approached. His face broke into a huge grin. He was missing several teeth.

"Care-REEEE! My dear! How *are we* today?"

"Just peachy, Harry. You got one of those for me?"

Carrie pulled out a one-dollar bill and handed it to Harry. In return, Harry handed her the thin newspaper.

"You be careful out here, Harry."

"Yes, ma'am. I certainly will."

Spare Change had been founded by a group of homeless individuals in 1992. Since its inception, the publication was credited with "giving homeless and economically disadvantaged people in the Greater Boston area a voice." More importantly, it provided those with low or no employment an opportunity to make a living as independent sales associates. Harry was one of the better-known salesmen for the paper. He had worked hard at it over the years, spending on average forty to fifty hours per week selling on the streets of Cambridge.

Harry concluded their transaction by tipping his hat. He then took a big bow. Carrie smiled. Suddenly, she was no longer thinking her earlier depressed thoughts about the lack of daylight, or about the failed experiment from earlier in the day.

Harry missed his calling, she thought. *He should have been a shrink.*

When Carrie had put some distance between herself and Harry, she pulled off her backpack and unzipped it. Then she stuffed the copy of the *Spare Change* newspaper in with the half-dozen or so other copies she had purchased over the past two days from other homeless street vendors. She would leave the copies of *Spare Change* in various labs and restrooms on campus for others to enjoy.

* * *

Carrie had just put the finishing touches on a PowerPoint presentation for the next day's seminar entitled "Discovery of a Novel Kinase Inhibitor Platform" when the subtle 'pop' from her email program sounded, followed by a popup message on her screen with the subject "attn.: C. Bloomfield." She didn't recognize the address, but the message had made its way past her aggressive spam filter so it was probably legitimate.

She clicked on the email. It read:

Dear Dr. Bloomfield:

I am Harold Kramer, a Senior Partner at Gately Winston Stewart & Washington, with offices in Providence, Rhode Island. Regretfully, I must inform you that Dr. Henry Winship who was employed at the Woods Hole Oceanographic Institute (WHOI) in Falmouth, Massachusetts passed away two weeks ago as the result of an apparent accidental drowning. He left no living relatives; his wife died two years ago.

Dr. Winship requested that, in the event of his untimely demise, our firm should forward to you a small shipping crate containing scientific materials that he believed you would find of great interest. Upon confirmation of this email, I will ship said package to you via Federal Express.

She shook her head in disbelief.

"Well, if that don't beat all."

Carrie repeated a phrase used often by her father, to her cat who was perched on the table next to the computer. In response, Sam sneezed all over the keyboard.

Carrie hadn't known Henry Winship well, but she and Henry had hit it off immediately after they first met at a seminar at Woods Hole a year before. Carrie felt that Henry was a kindred spirit of sorts. Like her, Henry dabbled in many different disciplines. His interests included oceanography, chemistry, biology, geology, as well as nutrition. He was a brilliant scientist. Apparently, the MacArthur Foundation thought so as well. Five years ago they had awarded him a "Genius Grant" of one million dollars.

Carrie recalled that they spent several delightful hours discussing one of his favorite topics: the incredible diversity of life at the bottom of the sea. It was Henry's belief that the pharmaceutical companies were missing out on a bountiful harvest by focusing almost exclusively on plant and animal life native to the rainforests of the Amazon and elsewhere. Instead, Winship maintained, industry scientists and researchers needed to expand their exploration of the deep and to examine the rich marine biology that lay far below. For it was from this cradle of life, believed Winship, that the future major breakthroughs in medicine and nutrition awaited discovery.

Several of Winship's colleagues considered his ideas nothing short of blasphemy. They argued that the Institute's mission should remain in the realm of "pure science." Indeed, a scientist's noblest purpose was the advancement of human knowledge. The men and women of WHOI were meant to be the caretakers—not exploiters—of the depths. The oceans were under constant assault by those whose motives were impure and based solely on financial reward. They opined that the new breed of scientific entrepreneur merely wanted to line his or her own pockets and rape the earth and the sea while churning out more consumer products and harmful technology.

From her brief discussions with Winship, Carrie learned he had begun to investigate the unique properties of some of the more exotic marine biology that he had recently discovered. His work was almost entirely self-funded, due in part to his MacArthur award but mostly, from his own personal fortune.

Through WHOI, Winship had access to an incredible underwater fleet of manned and robotic submersibles, including the Institute's best-known vehicle, *Alvin*. Earlier that year, Winship had personally piloted Alvin's successor *Simon* down to depths in the Pacific Ocean of over 18,000 feet. While at those depths, Winship had witnessed incredible sights: exotic Tubeworms that lived near hot vents on the ocean floor; unnamed creatures that could only be described as large, mutated jellyfish; and prehistoric-looking fish with gigantic jaws that spouted glowing red tentacles used to gather small fish and other animals in for food. When Winship had described the physical appearance of those horrific creatures to Carrie, she recalled thinking that they would have been right at home on one of H.R. Giger's movie set—alongside his other *Aliens*.

She recalled a conversation she had with Henry by phone just a few months earlier. He breathlessly told her he had actually managed to bring back some fragile samples from that *other* world, and his analysis of their chemical makeup had yielded some surprising results.

Carrie emailed a reply to the law firm expressing her condolences, along with instructions to send the package in care of the Yu Lab at the Whitehead Institute. Carrie was very sad to hear about Henry, but she was also curious to know what he might be sending her and why. Carrie knew that Henry didn't have any family, or close collaborators at WHOI. Moreover, he could be abrasive at times when expressing his opinions. She thought it sad: *I'm probably the closest thing Henry had to a friend.*

Although she and Henry had spoken only two or three times since the conference, Carrie thought that she must have made a much greater impression on him than she realized.

What the hell could he be sending me?

Carrie also thought it curious how the scientist had met his demise. She recalled that when they had first met, Henry had told her that he was an expert swimmer.

Didn't he hold several advanced lifeguard certifications?

CHAPTER FOUR

Run!

She was running as fast as she could. From "it," whatever "it" was. Her heart beat wildly as she raced into the darkness ahead. The footing was wet and treacherous. She stumbled, nearly falling several times. It was gaining on her. She could hear the gurgling noise getting louder by the second. Soon it would be upon her. As the sound grew to a roar she knew it was now or never. She had to stand her ground. She turned around to face her attacker, holding up both her arms in front of her body to shield herself from the thing pursuing her. She wanted to scream, both out of self-defense and sheer terror, but the scream seemed stuck in her throat...

"Prrrrrrrrrrrr...ah-CHOO!"

Samantha Elizabeth Bloomfield, II—Sam for short—was pressed up closely against Carrie's ear. She ceased her sonorous purring in order to let out a horrendous sneeze, waking up Carrie from the awful nightmare and covering the left side of Carrie's face with cat phlegm.

"Jesus Christ, Sam! What the hell?!"

The cat jumped quickly off the bed. Carrie sighed. She had to cut the fur ball *some* slack. After all, the tests she herself conducted on the large Siamese feline indicated that Sam suffered from a single allergy: she had a very marked reaction to flakes of skin and dandruff from Carrie herself.

* * *

Carrie locked the front door to her apartment and wheeled her street bike onto the sidewalk. Fall was in the air; it was a crisp November morning in Central Square, or, as she liked to call it, "02139-land." She would begin her trek on Broadway Street and then pedal down to Ames Street eventually reaching the M.I.T. Center for Cancer Research. Of the many haunts she visited, the Center was one of Carrie's favorites. She had worked there as a postdoctoral fellow almost thirty years ago.

In truth, Carrie didn't have to live in the small, cramped, nine hundred-square-foot, third floor apartment in this working class neighborhood of Cambridge. The wealth she had acquired from the royalties and licensing of her inventions would easily have allowed her to own a nice home in one of the affluent suburbs west or north of Boston. In addition, she could have afforded a spectacular vacation property on the Cape or the Vineyard. But Carrie genuinely loved the city and the people who inhabited it. Since arriving in Boston from Madison, Wisconsin, in the early 80s to attend graduate school at Harvard, Carrie had considered Cambridge to be her home.

Carrie believed in keeping a small carbon footprint. She walked, biked, or rode on the MBTA to go wherever she needed. If the situation dictated—say, a longer trip or a tight schedule—Carrie could avail herself of a short term rental car strategically situated nearby.

Although not a vegetarian, Carrie found herself gradually drifting into the lifestyle. Over the years, she had begun to cut back on red meat. Nowadays, she even avoided chicken. Carrie still ate fish, along with many of the tofu and grain-based meat substitutes. Some of them were actually quite tasty and sometimes Carrie had a hard time telling them apart from the real deal. At a recent Boston Vegetarian Food Festival, she sampled many of the vendors' offerings. She also purchased two new vegetarian cookbooks. To Carrie, it didn't seem like much of a stretch to cut out meat entirely from her diet. Still, she did have some nagging concerns about nutritional deficiencies that might arise if she avoided meat entirely. She wasn't sure that vitamin supplements could make up the deficit, especially when it came to Vitamin B-12. But Carrie was willing to conduct the experiment and see.

Carrie also felt it was important to minimize the cruelty perpetrated upon animals in the world. She preferred to contribute to the cause in her own way, through kind deeds and personal sacrifice. For example, she avoided using products of any cosmetic companies that were known to employ animal testing. She also made generous donations to groups whose actions made sense to her, both politically and ethically.

Carrie had strong feelings about the People for the Ethical Treatment of Animals. In her mind, PETA consisted primarily of "nut jobs" that were hell-bent on using violence and intimidation to accomplish their aims. Carrie had learned first-hand as a graduate student that PETA followers considered any legitimate scientific research involving animal subjects as fair game against which PETA should launch attacks.

Many years earlier, Carrie was cornered by an angry mob of protesting PETA supporters on the sidewalk along Longwood Avenue outside of the Harvard Medical School. Under the guise of "We'd like to talk with you for a moment," the mob began to pepper her with questions like, "If you had to sacrifice an innocent animal in order to cure a disease, would you do it?" Carrie, of course, naïvely replied in the affirmative. Her explanation was quickly drowned out with more questions from the crowd: "Do you work in a lab here?" "Do you work with animals?"

When she could get a word in edgewise, Carrie replied, "Yes, I work in Building C. And no, I don't work with animals."

This seemed to take the steam out of her inquisitors. The group backed away, and then started migrating down the street—presumably to look for other victims. Carrie was relieved, but she was also pissed.

"Hey!" she yelled at them. "Do you know that I slaughtered millions of bacteria today!? What do you think of that? Huh?!"

Some in the group shot her dirty looks but, by and large, they didn't seem to care what she had killed, so long as it wasn't the cute, four-legged, furry variety.

"Speciesists," Carrie angrily muttered to herself, as she walked away.

* * *

Carrie was wrapping up a meeting with members of Dr. Larry Stewart's lab. After the formal portion, some in the group had stayed behind to participate in an ad hoc discussion led by Carrie. She shared with them her current work on a promising new cancer diagnostic she had been developing currently in Phase I trials. She headed to Larry's office to pick up her backpack.

For years, Carrie had followed Stewart's work on yeast metabolism—in particular, how yeast could adapt to stressful environments. Yeast was an essential research tool in developing models for fighting cancer, and Larry Stewart's lab had added greatly to the underlying scientific knowledge base over the years.

As Carrie started to turn the corner out of Stewart's office, she couldn't help but overhear a conversation outside between two graduate students, a young man and woman both in their early 20s. It sounded to Carrie as if she were the subject of their conversation. The man was talking. The woman was giggling. The man said something that Carrie couldn't hear. The woman said, in response:

"Shut up! No way! She's not a lesbian."

"Oh yeah? How much you wanna bet? She's *definitely* a bull dyke. Everybody knows it. Look at her haircut, and the nose stud. Have you noticed how muscular her arms are? And how flat chested she is? She probably spends every waking moment of her spare time ogling women at the gym, and hanging out in the Diesel Café in Davis Square."

The man said something else Carrie couldn't make out. The young woman replied:

"Well, I hear she's a genius. Larry is certainly smitten by her, that's for sure. Did you know she has *three* Ph.D.s? And they say she's worth millions."

Carrie was annoyed and also slightly amused by the banter. But she had heard enough about herself. She cleared her throat loudly, and then casually stepped out from behind the doorway.

"One, actually."

The two students look at each other, horrified.

"*You* know—PhDs. They're actually not *that* fun to collect."

Stunned silence.

"Just one. From Harvard."

Finally the young woman spoke.

"Uhhh…Dr. Bloomfield. I…I'm really sorry. Please forgive us."
She turned and looked at her colleague. "We didn't mean any
disrespect."

"Apology accepted," said Carrie. "But I'd be a little more careful
about gossip in the future. You never know who or *what* may be lurking
just around the door. It could be someone from whom you'll be seeking
a letter of reference someday."

Carrie smiled at the woman. Then she turned and faced the
young man. Carrie wore a serious expression; her voice took on a tenor
of dramatic excitement.

"Or, *perhaps*…standing behind the door…it *could* be…a ho-
mo-SEXual!!!"

Ashamed, the man stared down at his feet.

"Ahh, Thao, it's Thao Nguyen, right?"

"Yes, ma'am—uh, Doctor."

"Thao, gosh, there's no need to be so formal. But, then again,
your name, Thao—it *does* means "courtesy," right? So, please do me this
small courtesy if you would please. I'd like you to tell all of those
everybodies that Carrie Bloomfield isn't a bull dyke. In fact, she doesn't
even qualify as a lesbian. But, they *are* right about a couple of things: she
is flat chested, and she *has* been known to work out in the gym—*and*
hang out at the Diesel Café."

* * *

That evening, Carrie ran into her neighbors and closest friends,
Edward and Terrance Smith-Hughes walking their miniature poodle,
Fee-fee, outside their building. After a few minutes of pleasantries, Carrie
shared with them the tale of her encounter earlier in the day with the two

graduate students.

"I told him, 'I'm not a bull dyke and I'm not gay but, of course, you're right about my being flat chested.' Then I told them, yes I *did*, in fact, hang out at the Diesel Café." Carrie started to laugh uncontrollably.

"Awesome!" said Terrance. "I would love to have been there to see the expression on their faces when you walked through the door."

"Well, believe me," said Carrie, "It was priceless. They looked like they both wanted to shrivel up and die from embarrassment." Carrie paused a moment from her laughter to wipe away the tears from her eyes.

"Honey," said Edward, "Don't you worry about batting 'right-handed.' You know we love you. And besides, you can be an honorary member of our team *any* day." He turned to his partner, Terrance, and slipped his arm around Terrance's waist and gave him a peck on the cheek. "Right, sweetie?"

Edward, Terrance, and Fee-fee occupied the second floor of the three-story house, directly below Carrie and her cat, Samantha. The gay couple was extremely devoted to one another. Edward was a successful artist and owner of a studio downtown; Terrance was a psychologist working for a small clinic providing services to low-income families in East Cambridge.

In the years she had known them, Carrie had come to love Terrance and Edward as brothers. She vividly recalled the early morning hours of May 17, 2004, when she had accompanied the proud couple to Cambridge City Hall. Edward and Terrance had become overnight celebrities, as the fifth same-sex couple to receive a marriage license issued by the Commonwealth of Massachusetts.

The midnight event garnered international media coverage, as tens of thousands of persons crowded onto the front lawn of City Hall to celebrate the legalization of gay marriage. The crowd was immense; it spilled out onto Massachusetts Avenue for several blocks.

Of course, all three of them had yelled themselves silly. Later that morning, during the wedding ceremony, Carrie proudly served as both bridesmaid and best man for the happy couple. She recalled how funny it was, hearing Edward and Terrance trying to exchange their vows. They were so hoarse; the two men could barely manage to croak out the words, "I do" in front of her, the clerk magistrate, and a witness.

"So, I guess you didn't get into the 'flat chested' stuff with them, huh?" Terrance asked Carrie.

Fee-fee barked at a cyclist riding down the sidewalk. Edward yanked on the dog's leash, imploring, "Hush, Fee-fee!"

"Nahh," Carrie replied, humorously. "I don't mind discussing my sexual orientation with people, but *some* things are off limits until the second date."

CHAPTER FIVE

Terrance Smith-Hughes thought it was time for his good friend Carrie to get out and circulate in the singles community and perhaps find that special someone. Both he and Edward knew it had been almost a year since Carrie had gone out on an actual date. They both (especially Terrance) were keen on tracking all aspects of Carrie's love life. Without asking her in advance, Terrance signed Carrie up for a speed dating session.

"Guys, I really appreciate your doing this. But—*speed dating? Really?*"

"Carrie, you'll love it sweetie," said Terrance. "Before I met Edward, I went to a few of them. They're fun! If nothing else, you'll meet a lot of interesting people. Besides, it's not like you *have* to sleep with any of them."

She looked at Edward. He smiled and then he shrugged his shoulders as if to say, *"Don't look at me. This wasn't my idea."*

* * *

Carrie hadn't had a clue what she should wear to an evening of speed dating. She showed Terrance a few of the items from her wardrobe she was contemplating.

"Yes! This is gorgeous!" He pointed to another item. "Yes. No, definitely *not* this. Yes, this is a *must*. It picks up the color of your eyes splendidly. Eww! This one, here," He motioned to a different blouse she had picked out, "has 'spinster' written all over it." He pointed to a different one. "I'd go with *this* blouse. It's not too provocative, but it's a teensy-weensy bit sexy, don't you think? Oh—and a very subtle shade of plum or mauve lipstick would match it perfectly."

"You *know* I don't wear lipstick! Get out of my bedroom, you scoundrel!" Carrie struck some mock blows against Terrance's shoulder.

In response, Terrance put on his best surprised-and-hurt look, and then he daintily tiptoed toward Carrie's bedroom door. Terrance blew her a kiss before closing it entirely. Carrie shook her head and grinned.

What in the world did I ever do before I met these guys?!

Carrie put on the skirt and blouse combination Terrance had recommended. She considered for a second using some perfume but then changed her mind. After fussing with her hair for a few moments, she went outside into the living room to present herself to Edward and Terrance for a final inspection.

* * *

"I'm 49 years old and I don't drink and I don't smoke. I've never owned a dog or a cat—my mother doesn't like animals—but that doesn't mean I wouldn't want to, someday. A stray from the pound might make a nice pet. Probably not a dog, though. You have to walk them every day. They can be very destructive, too. When I was growing up…"

A part of Carrie was still wondering how she had let Terrance talk her into this crazy shenanigan. If she weren't so embarrassed that she was attending, she'd probably find it quite hilarious! *Oh—I'll make him pay for this.*

Carrie was finding it increasingly difficult to focus on the monologue of her current date, "Joe." She wanted badly to look over and sneak a peek at the clock on the wall to see if five minutes were even *close* to elapsing. That would be cruel, though. No, she was determined to grin and bear it. Despite his quirks, Joe was probably a very nice guy. Nicer than the last guy, for sure. No doubt there was probably a gal out there somewhere whom Joe would make very happy someday. But not Carrie.

Carrie decided at the beginning of the evening to avoid saying anything about herself that might be considered self-aggrandizing. While Joe droned on about his childhood, Carrie ticked off in her mind the attributes of the last man, named Dave, with whom she had interacted.

Now, there's *a guy who could stand to learn a little humility!*

Physically, Dave was a hunk. But, alas, he would receive a failing score as a human being on her report card. Dave worked downtown as a financial advisor for one of the big brokerage companies. He described to her in great detail the nice home he owned in Weston, and the expensive sports car that he drove to weekend rallies. Carrie also learned that Dave had graduated at the top of his class from Yale. She had waited to see if he was going to reveal to her his actual grade point average. At one point during their five minutes together, she thought that Dave had actually flexed his muscles to her!

That guy has narcissist written all over him.

Carrie was convinced that any attempt to make a favorable impression with Dave would have been for naught. Carrie tried to not make snap judgments about people, but, in the first thirty seconds of their date Carrie decided she did not like Dave. He cared far more about where people went to school or what they owned or whom they knew or where they lived, instead of who they were inside or what they believed in. Carrie was struck by Dave's frown, and his loss for words upon learning that Carrie lived in a small apartment in Central Square.

"Oh," was his sole response, then silence, followed by more conversation about himself.

Of course Carrie neglected to tell Dave that she *owned* the biotech startup that employed her. She also omitted the fact that her current accumulated net worth was probably greater than what a high-powered financial analyst like him would earn over the course of his entire lifetime.

After saying goodbye to Joe, and watching him shift to the next table, she was joined by her next date. He was tall, medium build with a dark complexion. He looked awfully young. But it was the man's eyes that struck Carrie immediately. Terrance would pester her later that night wanting to know, "What color were his eyes?" but Carrie could not recall. She remembered only that they looked "kind."

She and the man dispensed with the typical "interview" format, and the boring "tell-me-about-yourself" routine. He asked her if she had a favorite artist. Carrie answered that she wasn't too familiar with many artists but she did tend to prefer the impressionists. As far as music, both had a mutual admiration for the work of John Coltrane. The man thought Coltrane was "the master." Carrie opined that "The Trane" reached his pinnacle after joining with Thelonious Monk and his band. Both thought that Coltrane had died far too young.

The two traded a short riddle, followed by some silly banter. Then he talked about how he liked to spend his evenings.

For Carrie, the five minutes passed far too quickly.

"Hey, I don't even know your name!" she said, after the timer ticked down to zero.

"It's Paul. Paul Santiago."

She smiled a genuine smile at him. "I'm Carrie. Carrie Bloomfield."

Paul gazed into her eyes as he shook her hand. Carrie was very aware that he held onto her hand for a few seconds longer than necessary. When he finished, Paul pulled out a business card. It was a homebrew affair containing a sketch of his likeness done in charcoal. On the back, Paul had written his phone number. As she turned it over, some of the charcoal rubbed off onto the palm of her hand.

"Sorry about that," he said. "Someday, when I've graduated beyond 'struggling artist' I'll have some real ones printed up. Carrie Bloomfield, eh? Call me sometime."

* * *

"Carrie, welcome! It's good to see you. How are you?"

Lisa Hartman, Ph.D., LCSW, motioned Carrie to sit in the

overstuffed leather chair a few feet from Hartman's own seat. A plump woman in her 60s, Dr. Hartman had maintained her practice in Somerville's Davis Square for twenty years.

"Good. I think." Carrie stopped to reconsider the authenticity of what seemed to her an automatic response. "Yes. Overall, I can probably—no, I can *honestly* say, 'good.' I think."

"Well, 'Good, I think' is as good a response as any. I think. So tell me, what's on your mind today?"

The two exchanged pleasantries for a few minutes. Eventually, Carrie opened up and talked to Hartman of her lack of a relationship in her life. No…it was a lack of interest in even *having* a relationship. She explained that it had been several years since her last sexual relationship, and thought of one evoked feelings in Carrie…feelings that were uncomfortable and a little scary—check that—they were a *lot* scary. She thought of the time spent with her old flame, Jim, back in the days of grad school. After that chapter of her life, Carrie was very much about control. And for Carrie, not being completely in control was an uncomfortable prospect.

"Something. I don't know. It almost feels as though my very competency is at stake. I guess a part of it is tied to the fact that, much of the time, I feel like a fraud. And the part of me that *does* feel real—well, I don't want to be robbed of that part. It could happen if I give myself over to loving someone. Or, if I allow him to love me."

"Well, Carrie, you *can't* stop someone from loving you. When you do love someone, they can possibly hurt you. But that doesn't mean you *shouldn't* love. Perhaps you should worry less about being hurt and instead, ask yourself, 'Is this person deserving of *my* love?'"

Carried paused for a second.

"That's a good point. I did meet a very interesting young man recently. That's the problem actually—he's *very* much younger. Also, we have so little in common professionally. He is an artist…I know so little about art. But, he's so upbeat and fun! I think it might be nice to get to know him better. To steal Jessica's line from *Who Framed Roger Rabbit*? 'He makes me laugh.'"

Carrie paused.

"But that's not enough of a reason to get into a serious relationship with someone, is it?"

"I don't know, Carrie. You tell me."

The two paused for a moment. Carrie mulled over the psychologist's last question, while Hartman took a sip from her cup of coffee.

"Carrie, tell me more about the part of you that feels like a fake. Actually, I think you described it as being a 'fraud,' right?"

* * *

Growing up, Carrie was used to always being the brightest person in the room. And because of this, she was frequently made fun of.

She was the "strange one." The "different one."

Carrie was a straight A student throughout high school and college. She took college-level courses during her senior year in high school. Her test scores were always through the roof.

"Nerd." "Geek."

The closest that Carrie ever got to spending time with the popular boys and girls—the athletes, jocks and cheerleaders—was when she tutored them. Although boys found her to be physically attractive, Carrie had unintentionally scared off more than one would-be suitor whose ego would simply not allow him to play second fiddle in the smarts department.

Carrie was never entirely convinced that she could out-think everyone. A part of her regarded herself as possessing normal—or, perhaps, only slightly higher-than-normal—intelligence. She couldn't come up with a plausible explanation for those sudden flashes of insight that she had. Sometimes it seemed as though they were born from snippets of dreams she remembered. Other times, intrusive thoughts would pop into her head. More accurately, they would seep into a corner of her mind, making themselves only peripherally noticeable—much like those annoying floaters that occasionally appeared in her field of vision.

All of her life, Carrie had felt as though she was faking it; the superior intellect that people constantly attributed to her wasn't real. It was merely the result of her unconscious channeling of something—or someone. It wasn't really her.

Sometimes, her anxiety got the better of her: her deepest fear would one day reveal itself—namely, that she was crazy. It wasn't so far-fetched: several family members on her mother's side—including her own mother—had suffered bipolar disorders.

* * *

The summer before she officially began her stint in graduate school, Carrie worked as a research assistant in one of the biochemistry labs at Harvard Medical School. One day, she spied a thin, newly bound book sitting on the lab bench near her desk. It contained the thesis of a recent Ph.D. student-turned post-doc, Carl Waxman. Waxman had just presented his work to his examination committee a few weeks before. Waxman was much relieved to pass his exams. It was the culmination of five years of hard, intensive research.

Intrigued, Carrie studied Waxman's thesis over her lunch break. Carrie then asked Waxman if she could borrow the copy and take it home with her to study further. The newly minted Ph.D. was flattered by her attention.

"Sure," Waxman told her. "Just don't lose it," he snickered. "There are only six copies in existence."

Carrie held on to the thesis for two days, during which time she critically examined his hypotheses and the experimental designs, along with the resulting data and Waxman's conclusions. Waxman's thesis advisor, Isaac Hubert, thought Waxman's thesis was a brilliant work of scholarly science. Hubert offered to employ Waxman as a postdoctoral fellow for one year until he found a more permanent position. Hubert was happy that Waxman was finally a member of the club but he was also genuinely proud of his student.

Carrie came into Professor Hubert's office the following day. She knocked meekly on his door.

"Am I disturbing you, Professor?"

"Not at all, Carrie. Come in, come in! What can I do for you?"

"If you have a few minutes, Professor, I'd like to discuss Dr. Waxman's thesis with you. I'm afraid I'm having difficulty accepting his conclusions. It's probably because I'm misunderstanding some key piece."

For the next half hour, Hubert and Carrie engaged in a highly technical discussion about Waxman's thesis. Carrie reviewed one section in meticulous detail.

Jesus, we should have had this girl on the examining committee!

Seeing that Hubert was growing restless—in fact, Hubert had half-risen from his chair to indicate that it was time for their meeting to come to a close—Carrie dropped a bombshell.

"I'll be quick, Professor. Do you see this experiment, here? The one where Dr. Waxman mixes together these compounds:

50mM TrisHCl(pH7.0); 5mM MgSO4; 0.5 mM ATP

"Yes."

Carrie had drawn Hubert's attention to the critical portion of Waxman's thesis—the one upon which the thesis's seminal conclusion was based.

"I asked Dr. Waxman precisely how these compounds were mixed, since he didn't actually describe the procedure in detail."

"Okay."

"Well, Dr. Waxman poured the compounds into a standard sized, 8x150mm tube and shook them vigorously, for approximately twenty seconds."

"And?"

"He sealed the top of the tube with his thumb."

"Okay. It's sloppy, I'll grant you that, but…"

Hubert still wasn't grasping the import of Carrie's revelation.

"Don't you see, Professor? These compounds? If they come into contact with the human body at a temperature of 37 degrees centigrade – the pH change that Dr. Waxman attributes to the function of the acyl carrier proteins…well, couldn't that merely be the byproduct of the heat from his finger and…"

Hubert, who had been standing up, plopped down in his chair, dumbfounded.

"Nebbish," he muttered.

"I…I beg your pardon, Professor. I didn't mean to offend."

"No. *Oh*, no! I didn't mean you, Carrie. *Certainly* not you."

He paused a moment to think. Finally, he said, "I would appreciate it if you wouldn't discuss this with anyone just yet. I need to have a little chat with our good Dr. Waxman."

CHAPTER SIX

"Please, can you spare some change, sirs?" the woman asked of the two college-age students as they walked by her on Massachusetts Avenue in Central Square. Ten years of living on the streets of New York and Philadelphia had been unkind to the woman. She appeared to be significantly older than her actual chronological age of thirty-five. Her clothes were worn, but clean. The woman had just arrived in Boston two weeks earlier, in search of a job. But it was hard going, especially without a permanent address or telephone to put on job applications.

The man closest to her sported a crew cut. His face bore a ruddy complexion. His clothes were fashionable, preppy-looking. Upon being addressed, the man stopped in his tracks. He ceased conversing with his buddy. Then he glared at the woman. Although the woman was used to receiving rude responses and heckling, this person seemed more threatening than most.

"See here, Gary! This is *exactly* what is wrong with this country. You have people like *this*…" He gestured at her, menacingly, "who are *too lazy* to look for jobs. Instead, they stand on the street corners and beg for handouts."

"I'm sorry, sir, I didn't mean to…"

"Yeah, man. I bet she gets a fat welfare check every month, courtesy Uncle Sam."

"Hey, lady, what did you score today? A hundred? Two

hundred? Gonna buy cigarettes and booze with it later tonight?"

She looked around. There wasn't anyone else nearby.

Just then, the man who spoke first reached out and grabbed her arm with one hand. With his other hand, he reached into her coat pocket and pulled out the contents. The woman's coin purse, along with a locket, and fifteen wadded-up one-dollar bills spilled onto the ground.

"Whadaya know, Gary? This broad's rich. She's got more money in her pocket than I have in my whole wallet right now. And she wants *my* money?"

The other man reached down and grabbed the locket. He opened it.

"Who's this, bitch?"

The locket contained a photo of a small child. The child appeared to be about a year old.

"That's probably your bastard grandson. Huh? Am I right?"

The woman replied, "Please, give that to me. You can keep the money. Just give me back the locket. Okay?"

The man dangled the locket in front of her. She made a grab for it, but the man jerked it away suddenly. He repeated the move. Again, she grabbed for it, unsuccessfully.

"Ah! Poor thing!"

"I'll give it to you if you dance for it. Com'on, bitch, dance for it!"

The man demonstrated by shuffling his feet to and fro in a comedic fashion.

The street person felt both terror and rage. She didn't know what to do. She started to tremble.

Just then, a woman on a bicycle approached the trio on the sidewalk. She stopped abruptly in front of them. Tall, middle-aged, and sporting a no-nonsense appearance, the newcomer turned and faced the homeless woman.

"Is everything okay here, Miss?" she asked.

"Butt out, lady," said one of the men.

The cyclist looked at the expression of fear on the woman's face. She dismounted from her bike and faced the duo eye-to-eye.

"I don't think so. In fact, you guys have about ten seconds to clear out of here before I kick *both* your asses, and then I'll call 9-1-1. Capish?"

The first man looked at his friend.

"Oh, this tough bitch…"

"YOU THINK I CAN'T DO IT?!" she shouted, angrily.

The man snarled at her, "Yeah, whatever. Go fuck yourself! You and your two-bit, piece-of-shit, gutter-slut friend here."

The two men walked away. As a parting insult, the man holding the locket heaved it into the street. The homeless woman ran out into the Massachusetts Avenue traffic to retrieve it. The car nearest her slammed on its breaks, narrowly avoiding hitting her. The driver angrily leaned on his horn for several seconds.

Meanwhile, the cyclist bent down and began to pick up the homeless woman's money. When the woman returned from the street, the cyclist handed it to her.

The homeless woman nodded in appreciation.

"Thanks. You didn't have to do that. They could have had a gun or a knife."

"I know," said the cyclist. "It was a gamble, but you look like the kind of person who would have done the same for me."

"Would you have?"

The cyclist looked at the homeless woman quizzically.

"Would you have 'kicked their butts?'"

The cyclist laughed. "I don't know. Maybe. I've never really tried." She added, "I *did* accidentally punch out one of my kid brothers once, when I was seventeen."

Her remark brought a smile to the homeless woman's face.

"Are you hungry?" asked the cyclist. "Can I get you anything?"

"Nah. I have this money. I was going to buy a burger and fries at McDonald's. Thanks, though."

"What about a place to sleep for the night? Are you set?"

"Yes, thanks. I'm headed down to the Winthrop Street shelter after I eat. I'll be fine. You've been very kind."

It was unusual when someone other than another street person—

or a homeless shelter worker—asked if she was hungry. Or cold. Or if she needed a place to stay. It was even more unusual for a complete stranger to stop and come to her rescue when she was being threatened.

And a woman, no less.

Although the homeless woman was more gun-shy than most street people, the kindness of this person motivated her to take a chance, and do something that was totally uncharacteristic for her: she reached out to give the cyclist a hug. The cyclist warmly embraced her in return. She held on to the woman for almost a half-minute; when they parted, the cyclist smiled kindly at her.

"Stay safe," she said. She got back onto her bicycle, and rode off.

"Hey! What's your name?"

The homeless woman watched the cyclist pedal down the street. It was beginning to get chilly. She put her hands in her coat pockets. She felt something unusual in the left-hand pocket. The cyclist must have slipped it in her pocket when they hugged. The woman pulled out the object. It was a wrapped turkey club sandwich.

* * *

Carrie Bloomfield received a top-notch education while at Harvard University. Her thesis advisor and mentor, Professor Patrick Seamus O'Connor, had taught and conducted biochemical research for over thirty years in his laboratory in Building C at the Harvard Medical School. During that time, O'Connor had schooled countless graduate students in classical biochemistry. It was a testament to O'Connor that so many of his former students had chosen professions in academia. And they, in turn, churned out new generations of talented researchers and teachers.

Patrick O'Connor was a *Doktorvater* in the true sense. Bright students—men and women like Carrie Bloomfield—presented themselves to O'Connor to be deemed worthy of his tutelage. They came to him as empty vessels, eager to be filled with his knowledge, experience, and scientific ethics. O'Connor honored this sacred obligation because he, too, had once sought out *his* Doktorvater among the ranks of an earlier generation of distinguished academicians—the colleagues of the very men who had fathered the modern science of biochemistry. Men like Sir Hans Kreps, Linus Pauling, and Fritz Lipmann.

O'Connor felt it was paramount to convey to his graduate students the joy and splendor that was inherent in the biological systems of living things. Indeed, O'Connor considered it a personal failure if *any* Ph.D. recipient left his lab feeling ambivalent about continuing on in a career in the life sciences. O'Connor left little to chance in his students' educations. He supervised them closely—working with them one-on-one for a portion of every day during the first few months of their apprenticeship, to ensure that they would have a thorough understanding of basic scientific procedures and lab safety.

All of the laboratories employed dishwashing staff to clean test tubes and glassware, and O'Connor's was no exception. What was different about his lab, however, was that each of O'Connor's graduate students was expected to spend a week working with the dishwashers so that they knew how to make glassware sterile, spotless, and reusable for their experiments. In addition to mastering basic scientific skills, O'Connor felt strongly that his young men and women needed to learn a certain level of humility along with an appreciation for the support and assistance they would receive during their tenure from the lesser-skilled members of the Harvard community. O'Connor wanted them to see *people*, not nameless faces. The stock handlers, the housecleaners, the dishwashers, and the secretaries; they were no less deserving of his students' respect just because they lacked a college diploma or they struggled with English as a second language. These decent, hardworking folks who called places like Mission Hill and Roxbury home made things work around the Medical School. And regardless of the menial tasks they performed, those men and women would indirectly contribute to the advancement of his students' scientific careers—just as they had contributed to O'Connor's.

Not surprisingly, more than one young researcher was unhappy with this facet of their education. They would decry that the dishwashing "course" was a complete waste of their time. And while they may have complained to the dishwasher, or their fellow students, they would never, ever have dreamt of doing so to Patrick Seamus O'Connor—or to the lab's "straw boss," Joanne Smiley, the senior lab technician. Smiley, a 29-year veteran who had begun her career with O'Connor on day one, was all-powerful; she could wilt a first-year grad student in his or her tracks with a single glare.

Carrie had not minded the dishwashing duties at all. She understood the importance of learning the basics. And she appreciated the fact that the lab worked together as a team. She paid careful attention during her training, for she soon realized that washing dishware properly was not as easy as it seemed. But Carrie soon mastered the tricks of the trade.

O'Connor's dishwasher was an older Hispanic woman who had worked for him for over fifteen years. Carrie found Maria to be extremely pleasant, with a cheery demeanor. Maria had liked the reserved, young Carrie; Carrie reminded Maria a bit of her own daughter. The two got along splendidly.

During her breaks, Carrie tutored Maria in English, drilling her in pronunciation, along with the proper use of pronouns and verbs. Carrie's favorite "textbook" was *The Boston Globe*. Maria, in turn, taught Carrie how to cook some classic Guatemalan dishes, and how to say a lot of swear words in Spanish. Carrie knew that one could never truly "grok" another's culture unless and until they had an appreciation for its national dishes and also, how to "swear like a sailor" in its native tongue. It seemed like a fair exchange.

One day, early into her training, Carrie was working alongside Professor O'Connor at the bench. She had been tasked with synthesizing a certain compound from five basic chemicals using only a shaker and the Bunsen burner. Most labs would have simply ordered the compound from a supply house. But to O'Connor, any scientist worth his or her salt should know how to synthesize from scratch roughly 80 percent of all of the compounds found in a typical laboratory.

Carrie was confident that she could produce a perfect product in the time allotted. She carefully laid out the raw materials. Next, she began

46

her notebook entry, writing down the experimental protocol. She would follow up with a subsequent entry to record the results. Carrie turned on the shaker. Next, she hooked up one end of a long rubber hose to the Bunsen burner's base, and the other end to the gas jet. All the while, Dr. O'Connor observed Carrie carefully.

Carrie started to turn on the spigot in preparation for lighting the Bunsen burner.

"Carrie, I trust you realize that…"

O'Connor did not have the opportunity to complete his observation. The rubber hose flew off the base of the burner, spraying O'Connor liberally with H_2O.

Carrie was horrified. She realized her mistake, and quickly turned off the gas—correction, *water*—but not until Prof. O'Connor's crisp, white lab coat had gotten thoroughly soaked – and he with it.

Professor O'Connor let out a brief sigh. Carrie stared at him, horrified; O'Connor's face was expressionless.

"If you'll excuse me, Ms. Bloomfield, I shall be in my office, where I will attempt to change into something more…dry."

O'Connor nodded to her, and then calmly stepped around her and out of the lab.

The following day, Carrie arrived at the lab bench to find that each of the spigots had been carefully labeled with masking tape and the words, "Gas" and "H_2O."

She never repeated that mistake.

* * *

A quarter of a century later, at Professor O'Connor's 90th birthday celebration, Carrie decided to broach the subject with the aging academician.

They exchanged a few minutes of pleasantries, after which O'Connor paid Carrie a nice compliment:

"You know, Carrie, you were, without question, my most gifted student. You were very passionate about the science. But more importantly, you cared so deeply about people."

Carrie blushed; she thanked her Doktorvater for his kind remarks, and paid him a high compliment in return:

"It was *you* who instilled in me that passion and love for science; to pursue the study of living things, Doctor. For that, I shall *always* be grateful."

She could see the beginnings of tears welling in the old man's eyes.

Carrie screwed up her courage, and inquired, "Doctor O'Connor? I hope you don't mind my asking after all these years. But, do you recall that day when I accidentally soaked you with water when I turned on the wrong spigot?"

"Yes, I do."

"Were you…angry with me?"

O'Connor chuckled. "Oh, heavens no, my child. I was trying so very hard to maintain my dignity, and to keep from bursting out laughing!"

CHAPTER SEVEN

"There's a package in the mailroom for you, Carrie. I signed for it."

The voice belonged to Leslie, a woman in her early forties, and one of the seasoned administrators at the Whitehead Institute for Biomedical Research. The researchers had nicknamed her "The Guardian of the Coffee." No one got even remotely close to the coffee pot without Leslie's say-so.

Leslie was holding out a clean mug for Carrie as Carrie walked up.

"Thanks, Leslie. You're a lifesaver. You know that, right?"

"So they say."

As she poured, Carrie asked, "Who's it from?"

"I'm not sure. But I think I recall seeing a Rhode Island return address."

Carrie remembered now. It was the package that Henry Winship's law firm had talked about. The former Woods Hole scientist had, for whatever reason, decided to send her a care package from *the great beyond.*

Carrie walked down to the mailroom and retrieved a crate. She sat down at her lab desk and pulled out a pair of side cutters from the toolbox in her drawer. She carefully clipped away at the metal straps securing it. Under the packing peanuts, Carrie found a handwritten note, a half-dozen DVDs, several lab notebooks, and sixteen large tubes filled with a light brown, gelatinous substance.

Carrie got out her laptop from her backpack, and popped in the first of the DVDs. Then she settled back with her coffee to peruse its contents.

Four hours—and one cold, half-drunk cup of coffee—later, Carrie was still glued to the computer screen.

* * *

Jacob Shapiro grew up in the 1950s as a skinny kid in the Jewish neighborhood of Mattapan in Boston, Massachusetts. His mother, Esther Shapiro, had aspirations for her only son to grow up and study for the Rabbinate. His father, Saul, only cared that the boy learn an honest trade and do well in life. Saul had run a small but successful kosher butcher shop on Blue Hill Avenue for thirty years. Friends would ask Saul, "Are you making a good living at the shop?" He would shrug his shoulders and reply in deadpan fashion, "Eh. I'm comfortable. But Esther will be the death of me yet."

At an early age, Jacob had a penchant for literature and the arts. The young boy's idea of the perfect Saturday afternoon was to ride the street car into Copley Square to the Boston Public Library, where Jacob would lose himself in the stacks, spending hours devouring dusty old manuscripts containing prose from the likes of 17th century authors like Simon Ockley, Antoine Galland, and Jonathan Swift.

His mother worried about a great many things in her life. In particular, she was worried that her boy would grow up to be a sissy. So, when Jacob turned thirteen, she enrolled him in one of the local Little League Baseball teams. Jacob hated the idea of being separated from his treasured authors and playwrights in order to play some "stupid game." Besides, he was no good at it. The ridicule he received from teammates made him feel all the more miserable. Jacob was constantly tormented. The other players inscribed a star on the bench with his name on it. Jacob was known as the team's "star benchwarmer." The few times his coach *did* take pity on the "scrawny little Jewish kid" and put him into the game in right field, Jacob would invariably have the misfortune of missing the one fly ball that allowed the other team to go ahead; or, swing on that last strike to cause the game-losing out. Those were not happy times for Jacob.

But life goes on, kids grow up, they escape their haunted pasts and eventually—if they're lucky—they find their niches. Jake flowered in college at Brown University; he excelled as a thespian and a student of the humanities, eventually going on to be named a Rhodes Scholar. After earning a doctorate in England, Jake toured with a theatrical production company, starring in several major productions off-Broadway. But at the age of 29, Jake made a major mid-course direction in his life: he decided to follow in his Uncle Bernard's footsteps and become a lawyer. Jake applied to, and was accepted at Harvard Law School.

* * *

Jake Shapiro, Esq., of Brack, Doyle and Peabody, was considered by his peers to be one of the brightest patent litigation attorneys in the country. He had been voted "Massachusetts Super Lawyer" for ten years running. Shapiro was in his mid-sixties, tall, with a full head of short-cropped, silver hair. His contemporaries said he was on the top rung of the ladder.

When Shapiro's iPhone started vibrating, he discreetly looked down under the table and saw that it was a message from Carrie Bloomfield. Carrie was on Jake's "short list," which consisted of only about ten persons who warranted his immediate attention, day or night. Hers was one of the few telephone numbers capable of triggering his phone during meetings.

Jake interrupted the speaker. "If you'll excuse me, ladies and gentlemen, I must take this call." The meeting had been in session for only five minutes. Jake slid back his chair, rose, and walked out on a full meeting of the managing partners of the firm.

"Hi Carrie, I got your text. To what do I owe the pleasure?"

"I hope I'm not disturbing you, Jake."

"Carrie, you know that you always have my full, undivided

attention. What can I do for you, today?"

Carrie explained to Jake about the email from Winship's law firm, and their instructions to send to Carrie the deceased scientist's mysterious package containing his work.

"Jake, I've been poring over Henry's data for nearly two straight days. Last night I could barely sleep. I dreamt about those chemical compounds. They danced in my dreams. They curtsied. They bowed. They whispered to me what they were capable of. This morning, I filled over twenty pages in my notebook with possible hypotheses and experiments. My hand is still cramping. And that's just the tip of the iceberg. The implications are—well, frankly I'm blown away. The results of the analyses Henry performed on these deep-sea samples are absolutely incredible."

Carrie continued, "I don't mean to sound paranoid, but I think I need to be careful with this. I'm not convinced that Henry died of natural causes. According to Henry's law firm, the Barnstable County Coroner's Office wasn't totally convinced, either. Even so, the D.A. ruled it as an accidental drowning—in record time, no less. Now, this is the strange part: the man told me he an *expert* swimmer. I mean, this guy instructed *lifeguards* how to swim, for Chrissakes."

Carrie stopped to catch her breath. Only then did she realize that she was talking much faster than usual.

"He writes in his cover letter to me that he's being followed, and that his office is bugged. Some outfit in Texas approached him, offering huge sums of money if he turned over to them all of his research on alternative energy. But Henry didn't want to go there. Besides, he didn't need the money; he was independently wealthy. What did he do? He left very specific instructions to his colleagues and lab staff to not acknowledge the existence of the samples or his work to anyone – not to any of the WHOI administration, inquiring media, and certainly not to any companies.

"Then—and this is where it gets really bizarre—he prepares a "dead man's switch" of sorts, a package containing his lab notebooks and specimens, which he updates on a regular basis. He left this package in the care of his karky fixers in Providence, with instructions to get the package to me in the event that he fails to contact them within a four-week window.

"Not only that—he gets his law firm to write a lengthy declaration of physical and intellectual property assignment, naming me as the assignee. Somehow, he and his firm managed to cut WHOI entirely out of it. Can you believe it?"

"It seems plausible, Carrie. Especially if the research was solely funded from his MacArthur Foundation grant money and his own fortune."

Jake paused for a moment.

"Here's what I want you to do…"

Jake instructed Carrie to make backup copies of all of the DVDs and notebooks. Then she should write and encode a summary of her potential inventions using strong encryption and transmit the file using the firm's virtual private network. She was to wait for two bonded couriers to arrive at her apartment at 7:00 PM. After the couriers had identified themselves, using a code phrase known only to themselves, Jake, and Carrie, Carrie would hand over the sensitive material for transport back to the law office.

"Don't let any research notebooks out of your sight, got it?"

"Roger that. Oh, Jake—have I ever told you that you're my favorite karky fixer?"

Carrie was fond of teasing him by using the slang reference to the lawyer in Heinlein's novel, *I Will Fear No Evil*. But Jake had his own description for her, too.

"Yes, many times, my dear lady. And, have I told you that you're my favorite goose who lays the golden eggs? Say, what are you doing for dinner next Tuesday evening?"

* * *

Growing up, Carrie Bloomfield had been a rambunctious little girl. At an age when most children played with dolls or G.I. Joes, she dabbled with chemistry sets and telescopes. Carrie did like to role-play in "pretend doctor" games with her little friends. Unfortunately, the rules of her doctor game landed her and her friends in hot water, causing considerable consternation with the adults.

On the sunny afternoon of May 8, 1965, Richard and Mary Bloomfield were called by Carrie's elementary school and asked to come in to the principal's office. The school secretary told them only that "Carrie was safe and unharmed" and that it concerned "an urgent disciplinary matter." They hurried over to the school. Waiting there also were two other sets of parents—Mr. and Mrs. Garfield, the parents of one of Carrie's closest friends, Tabatha; the other set, Mr. and Mrs. Stevens, who were the parents of a neighborhood boy, Philip. Philip played occasionally with little Tabatha and Carrie.

"Mr. and Mrs. Bloomfield, Mr. and Mrs. Garfield, and Mr. and Mrs. Stevens, thank you for coming in today," began the stern-looking Margaret Jenkins, the school's principal. "Let me begin by saying that we at Howard Ross Elementary School hold our children to the highest standards of conduct and civility." She paused for a moment to allow the gravity of her words to sink in. All six parents looked at one another, perplexed.

"We expect and encourage our boys and girls to be curious about the world around them, and we even tolerate—up to a point—questions about…ahem…their own bodies."

A look of alarm spread to the faces of Mrs. Stevens and Mrs. Garfield. Richard and Mary, however, remained calm.

"Mr. and Mrs. Bloomfield, I understand that your daughter, Carrie, may be the instigator of this unfortunate incident."

Finally, Richard Bloomfield spoke up.

"Ms. Jenkins, I'm at a total loss here. Would you please explain to us what exactly our children have been up to, and why we are here? I'm sure there's some rational explanation."

"Mr. Bloomfield, it might not be appropriate to discuss this matter in front of the others. Perhaps…

Just then, Tabatha's mother interrupted.

"Please! Please, Ms. Jenkins. You're frightening us. Would you please answer Mr. Bloomfield's question? Has there been any…inappropriate touching?"

Ms. Jenkins finally explained to the worried parents that little Carrie, Tabatha, and Philip had been observed during the lunch hour playing "doctor." Carrie had designated herself as doctor, while Tabatha played the role of receptionist/nurse. The role of patient fell upon Philip. After being brought before the doctor by Nurse Tabatha, Philip was subjected to a lengthy question and answer "interview" with which "Dr." Bloomfield attempted to ascertain the source of Philip's symptoms. With able assistance from her trusted nurse, the doctor next requested that her patient supply her with a urine sample. Little Philip obliged by peeing into a Dixie cup, which Tabatha then sealed with Saran wrap. Carrie took the sample home for analysis using the chemistry set her father had bought her for her last birthday.

"SHE DID *WHAT*?!?" roared Bloomfield.

"Mr. Bloomfield, she…"

Ms. Jenkins never got the chance to clarify her remarks. Richard Bloomfield began to laugh uncontrollably. His belly laugh doubled him over and for a few seconds, robbed him of the ability to take a breath of air. He wheezed. Tears came to his eyes.

The two other fathers in the room also started laughing hard. In seconds, the tension in the room had disappeared completely. Everyone in the room was smiling—everyone that is, except for Principal Jenkins.

Mr. Bloomfield, you may think this is a laughing matter but I can assure you…"

"Come on, Mary," said Richard, cutting her off in mid-sentence. He was trying very hard not to lose control again. Let's grab Carrie and go for some ice cream! Folks, you're welcome to…join…" But he couldn't finish the sentence, nor could he control himself. "…joi… HA-HA-HA-HAAAAA!"

* * *

Carrie Bloomfield was born in Los Angeles, California but grew up in Madison, Wisconsin. She was born into a family of an older sister, followed by two brothers. Her mother, Mary, died when Carrie was twelve. Carrie's father, Richard Bloomfield, was a successful engineer-turned-manager. He worked for almost twenty years with Northrop Grumman before deciding to move his family away from L.A. and back to his hometown of Madison, Wisconsin. There, Bloomfield taught physics at the University of Wisconsin. The widower never remarried; he retired in 2001 at the age of 74.

The oldest of Carrie's brothers—William—still lived near Madison. He was 44 years old. Twice divorced and a carpenter by trade, William had two children from his first marriage. His second marriage was childless and lasted a little less than one year. William had better luck with his third wife, Karen; they had been together now for almost six years. In 2009, when it appeared that the couple would be unable to conceive a child, William and Karen adopted a four-year-old girl from the Philippines. Theirs was a happy family.

Her younger brother, Earl, attended UCLA, graduating with a degree in business. After college, Earl stayed on the west coast. He worked as a buyer at a major software company in Silicon Valley. Single, but quite active on the dating scene, Earl never seemed to find the time to write or call his father, brother or sister. He maintained a Facebook account however, and on rare occasions would actually post content— mostly stuff about his softball team at work, or photos of his latest girlfriend. Carrie felt as though she knew Earl only through a tenuous electronic thread over the 'net. In contrast, Carrie enjoyed regular contact with her father, her brother-in-law, and her brother William and his family.

Carrie's heart still ached for her older sister, Samantha. The two girls had shared not only a bedroom while growing up but also, all of their dreams and aspirations. There was a four-year difference in their ages, but the two were nevertheless inseparable. Samantha pursued a degree in Economics at U.W., but after two years she dropped out of college and married her high school sweetheart. They had two children together. Samantha died at the age of thirty-nine from breast cancer—the same, hideous disease that had claimed the life of their mother, Mary, when she was roughly Samantha's age.

As a professional in the life sciences, Carrie was keenly aware that she, too, was at high risk for developing breast cancer. Not only was there the family history to consider; Carrie had tested positive for mutations in the BRCA1 gene. Her choices were clear enough: do nothing, and gamble that she might get lucky and cheat death; or, undergo a preventive mastectomy. To Carrie, the choice was a no-brainer. As much as she wanted to be "normal" and retain what society deemed an essential element of femininity, Carrie preferred instead to stay alive. After a few days of contemplation and meditation, Carrie called Massachusetts General Hospital to schedule the surgery. She would undergo a bilateral mastectomy: the removal of both her breasts.

Carrie was forty-one years of age. She was never more frightened in her entire life. Or more determined.

CHAPTER EIGHT

Several weeks had elapsed since Carrie had attended the speed dating event that her best friend Terrance Hughes-Smith had arranged. Paul Santiago, the young, handsome artist, had intrigued Carrie. And although she hadn't called him, she was still carrying around his homemade business card in her wallet.

"Carrie, why don't you give him a call?" asked Terrance. "You said you liked him."

"I don't know, Terrance. Yes, I thought he was very dashing— and a lot of fun—and even charming."

"Okay, so—where's the 'but'?"

"The 'but'? The 'but' is—*my God*! He looks like he's in his late twenties. Don't you see? I'm probably older than his mother!" said Carrie, exasperated.

"Carrie, no one's talking marriage here. What's wrong with being friends with a younger guy? Besides, he may be in need of a 'Mrs. Robinson.'"

"You're outrageous, do you know that?" Carrie responded.

"Bwak! Bwak!" Terrance squawked, while making flapping motions with his arms.

"Okay, okay. Yes, I…I guess I am a little chicken. I'm afraid of rejection. What if he decides it was a huge mistake to get involved with me? It's the probable outcome." Carrie added, "He'll soon figure out that we have nothing in common. After all, I know almost *nothing* about the arts. And what if he thinks I'm only, like, 40-something—and then I tell him I'm really 53, huh?"

"Honey," said Terrance, calmly, "He *gave* you his card! You showed it to me that night, remember? It was a work of art! That *has* to prove he doesn't think you're an old hag. Speaking of his card—you still *have* it, don't you?"

"Yes."

"Good. Because if you don't use it right now and call him, I'm gonna take it from you and call him myself. If he resembles *anything* like his sketch, then he's gorgeous."

"Uh, Terrance—I have no doubt that you can charm the socks off of any straight man, but aren't you afraid of hurting Edward's feelings?"

"Oh, hush up! You know I'd share him with Edward. Now go get his card."

Carrie shook her head as if to say 'you're impossible' but she did as she was told. The charcoal sketched image of Paul's likeness was almost completely rubbed off but, fortunately, Paul had written his phone number on the back in ink. She studied it for a few seconds.

"Well?"

"Well what? I'm *not* going to call him in front of you, Terrance! A lady's got to have *some* dignity. And besides, he probably doesn't even remember me. Don't worry. I'll come down in a little while and give you two a full report. Now, scat!"

* * *

Carrie knocked on Terrance and Edward's door about twenty minutes later.

"Come in, come in!" Edward greeted Carrie and handed her a freshly baked chocolate chip cookie.

"Umm! These are delicious," Carrie remarked.

"So, you're smiling, and I'm sure it's not simply because of Edward's scrumptious cookies. Tell it *all*, girl!"

"Well, he remembers me. I guess I made some kind of impression on him. When I told him who I was, it sounded as though he almost spilled a glass of something."

The gay couple looked at each other, both with big grins on their faces. "That's excellent! You startled him. I bet he's been pining away for that call," said Edward. "Don't you feel bad now, you made him suffer all this time?"

"Well, maybe."

Carrie took another bite from the chocolate chip cookie.

"We had a nice chat. If Paul was bothered that I waited to call, he was polite enough to not say so. We're getting together Saturday for a walk around Fresh Pond. It's not really a date. Well, perhaps a *pre-date* date."

"Uh-huh," remarked Terrance. He was grinning, again. "Call it what you want, darling, but I bet he has a serious crush on you. Now, be sure to play a *little* hard to get, okay?"

"Yes, he's absolutely right," said, Edward. "You definitely don't want to let him get you into the sack until the post-pre-date."

"Shut up, you two!" They all three giggled.

* * *

It was a cool, cloudless December morning as Carrie and Paul Santiago walked together around Fresh Pond in Cambridge. They had just finished a brunch buffet at the hot food bar at the nearby Whole Foods Store on the Parkway, after which they walked over to Fresh Pond. The two power-walked past the golf course and arrived at the smaller Lilly pond, where dogs were allowed to bathe. Several dogs— both small and large—were jumping in to fetch sticks tossed in by their owners. Then, they would run up to their owners, drop their sticks, and proceed to shake themselves dry—soaking their owners in the process. It was great fun for both dog and dog owner. For the non-dog owners like Carrie, it was amusing to watch as well.

Paul asked her, "Do you suppose there are more dogs than there are people out here today?"

"It's a distinct possibility. I wonder when Cambridge will start issuing licenses to persons to be here, as they do for dogs."

"Yes, license the *people* so the dogs can walk them. I like it! This is truly a wonderful place, Carrie. And you say the city gets its water from here? Not from the Quabbin Reservoir?"

"That's right," she replied.

Carrie decided that it was time to broach the subject about their respective ages.

"Paul, how old do you think I am?"

"Is this a trick question?" he chuckled.

"No, it's just that you might be surprised to know how old I actually am. My friends say I look a lot younger than my actual age."

"Well, let me see now." Paul stopped in his tracks. Carrie did likewise. Paul pretended to examine her closely. He started first by gazing into her eyes. He then playfully scanned the rest of her body.

"Give me your hands."

"What?"

"Give me your *hands*. You wanted me to guess your age, right?"

Carrie smiled. She held out both of her hands to Paul, who started touching each. He first stroked her fingers, and then he turned them over and stroked the palms. He encircled her wrists, and slid his hands up her arms a few inches. Finally, with his eyes closed, he reached up and stroked Carrie's cheek with his hands. He continued to keep them closed.

"I'd say that you're…you're…53."

"What?! How did you…?"

"Hey, what can I say? You're pretty well known in this town. I googled you.

"I bet you enjoyed that—all that touching, didn't you?" asked Carrie, amused.

"Oh, very *much* so." Paul said. "You have to admit, it's a good ice breaker."

Carrie and Paul resumed walking. The two separated in order to dodge a large black Labrador retriever that was headed straight for them.

"Lucky! Come back here!" the owner cried ahead to his dog

who had slipped his leash. When the owner had passed, Carrie and Paul rejoined one another on the path.

"So you knew I was considerably older than you, but you were still hoping I'd call?" asked Carrie.

"Carrie, this may come as a shock to you, but I don't care *how* old you are. I like *who* you *are*. *Inside*. And now that I've had an opportunity to get to know you better, I like the *outside*, too. Besides, I have the feeling you're a young person at heart."

"Okay, now that you've gotten to know the 'outside' of me better, are you going to reciprocate and let me guess your age, too?"

* * *

Carrie was not too far off the mark following her physical examination of Paul Santiago. They sat on a bench along the path. With her eyes closed, Carrie touched Paul's face and noted how soft his clean-shaven face felt. She enjoyed the shape of the dimples on his cheeks.

"You know that dimples are thought to be genetically inherited, right?"

"I did not know that!"

"Yes, and they're caused by variations in the structure of the facial muscle known as zygomaticus major. It's a simple dominant trait."

"Fascinating! But you're stalling, Dr. Bloomfield. Is there any *other* part of me you'd like to touch? Or, do you care to make a guess now?"

"I'd like to 'Phone-A-Friend."

"Beep! Sorry, your call cannot be completed as dialed. Please hang up and make your guess. This is a recording."

"Okay," replied Carrie. "Here goes. But keep in mind I haven't had the benefit of googling you, so I could be off by a decade. Or two. Okay?"

"Okay."

"Twenty-eight."

"Not bad!" replied Paul, with genuine surprise. "I'm actually twenty-seven. But who's counting?"

"Well, I am. But you have to tell me the truth, Paul—am I older than your mother?"

"Sorry to disappoint you, Carrie, but no. I came along late in life."

"Phew!" said Carrie. "I feel a whole lot better."

* * *

Paul and Carrie's pre-date went so well, they agreed to have a real dinner date. Carrie suggested Legal Seafood in Kendall Square. She told Paul that she would go out with him on one condition: the two would split the bill. Paul agreed.

They met around 7:30 p.m. and had drinks. After they were seated, Paul ordered the shrimp, while Carrie had baked scrod. The two split popcorn shrimp and clam chowder.

"So, what else did you learn when you googled me, Paul?"

"Not as much as you might think. I got your CV along with a long list of scientific papers. The age thing—well, I had to put a couple of information sources together to come up with that."

Paul took a sip from his Sam Adams Octoberfest, and then he continued.

"You know, I was quite impressed with all the different research institutes that mention you by name. I know that you were in industry for a number of years, but then your name starts popping up at an institute here, and a lab there. I was beginning to wonder if perhaps there were several Carrie Bloomfields, and I was confusing them for a single person."

Carrie laughed. "It's a long story. Let's just say that I don't like to be tied down to a single institute or company. But you're right, too, about there being more than one Carrie Bloomfield."

"Ooh, this sounds mysterious!"

"It could be," she replied. "I suppose my life is certainly more complicated than what you'll learn about me on Google. Just ask my two best friends in the world, Terrance and Edward. Incidentally, they're dying to meet you. It was their idea to sign me up on the speed dating thing."

"I'd like to meet them. Perhaps they'll be able to shed some light on the inscrutable Carrie Bloomfield. Or, are the other Carrie Bloomfields a mystery to your closest friends as well?"

"Probably not."

Carrie decided to change the subject.

"Tell me about your family, Paul. You said that you are of Spanish heritage. Are you from a big family?"

"Yes, indeed," replied Paul. Two brothers and two sisters. "We go back only two generations in America. My grandfather and grandma hopped off the boat from Chania in Crete back in 1934. They settled in New Jersey. Our family has been there ever since. With the exception of one cousin, I'm the first to leave the state."

"Wow. That must have been a bit of a shock for your family."

"Yes, I suppose it was. But it wasn't the biggest shock. My mother set that record when she married a Spaniard. There—I've said it. I'm a 'mutt.'"

They both laughed. Paul upended his glass. The waiter came over and asked if Paul wanted another. He nodded affirmative.

"How about you, Carrie? From my *extensive* research online, I know that you're from the west coast."

"Me? Born in the City of Angels, but raised in the cornfields of Wisconsin. My father moved the family back to the Midwest when I was little. I have no idea how many generations my roots go back in that state."

The time went by at an amazing clip. Before Carrie knew it, it was almost 11 p.m. They had discussed a great many things, including Carrie's whacky friends. She warned Paul that he might find their behavior—and their questioning—embarrassing.

"They're just trying to look out after my best interests, Paul. You see, they think that they're better judges of what constitutes a sexy, handsome, attractive man than I."

"And are they?"

"No. But I let them think that. Oh, and just so you're forewarned

—you should know that I let them pick out clothes for me."

"You wha…!?" Paul started to laugh, but then he snorted beer up his nose and began coughing.

"Sorry." Carrie giggled in response. "I kid you not. That outfit you saw me wear to speed dating? Terrance picked that out. He's afraid that I'm going to end up as an 'old spinster' if he doesn't intervene in the wardrobe department."

"Cute," Paul said.

"That's funny. That's *exactly* what they think about you."

"What?"

"They think you're cute. I warn you—they'll try and hit on you. But don't worry. I've decided that I'm not willing to share."

* * *

After dinner, Carrie went back with Paul to his apartment in Somerville's Union Square. Paul lived in a tiny unit even smaller than Carrie's.

"You'll have to forgive me. The place is a mess."

Paul's apartment was, in fact, cluttered, but it was also very organized. Art materials: an easel, paints, brushes, and pens were in evidence everywhere. Paul put on "Interstellar Space" by John Coltrane on his small stereo. Carrie was sure she had heard it once before even though she did not own that album.

Paul reached over and begun massaging Carrie's back with one hand. She didn't object. It felt great. After a moment, Paul shifted on the couch and began using both hands.

"Did you know, you feel awfully tense?"

"No, but I'm not surprised. My life has been somewhat hectic of late. But…Mmmm. Keep doing that, whatever you're doing. It feels won-der-ful!"

After a few moments, Carrie closed her eyes. She felt totally relaxed. She decided to strategically rest her right hand on Paul's upper thigh. In response, Paul gently caressed Carrie's neck. Then he leaned over and kissed the back of her neck. Then behind her left ear. Carrie let out a sigh.

It wasn't too long until both were passionately kissing. Carrie extrapolated that Paul was a very good lover, if his kissing skills were any indication.

Between kisses, Paul said, "You'll…mmm…you'll protect me…mmm…from your…friends…mmm?"

"Mmmm…absol…mmm…lutely," she replied.

Ten minutes later, Paul suggested that they might be more comfortable in the bedroom. Carrie agreed. They lay down on his futon mattress and fully embraced one another. They kissed some more. After a while, Paul took his shirt off. He looked at her with anticipation.

Carrie suddenly became quiet. Paul sensed that he might be pushing things faster than she was comfortable with. He started to apologize.

"No—sssshhhh." She pressed her finger up against his lips.

"It's okay. Remember, you joked earlier about Carrie Bloomfield being a woman of mystery?"

"Yes."

Carrie thought: *Better for him to know now, instead of later.*

She turned her back to Paul and began unbuttoning her blouse. As she unbuttoned, she said,

"Well, one of my many mysteries may come as a big shock. It's lost me a lover or two over the years. What I'm about to show you, Paul—if this freaks you out, I won't think any less of you. I should have mentioned it from the very beginning."

Carrie turned back to face Paul, naked from the waist up.

Paul's eyes grew big.

Here it comes.

"WOW!" exclaimed Paul. "Wait here a second."

"What?!" she asked.

"I have to grab my sketchpad. I've never seen such an amazing tattoo in my entire life! Who *created* this masterpiece?!"

Carrie was dumbfounded. She wasn't sure which was more shocking—Paul's fascination upon seeing her amazing "canvas" or his complete lack of concern over her scarred, breastless body.

Several minutes passed. She could hear Paul rummaging around in the living room closet for a sketchpad. Exasperated, she undressed completely and awaited his return.

CHAPTER NINE

After receiving Winship's package, Carrie had spent many of her waking hours studying its contents. The content in the lab notebooks was fascinating. The DVDs contained backup copies of the notebooks, and also a multitude of photographs and extensive background material from various publications describing what was known about the marine life forms that Winship and his colleagues had encountered during their dives. She wondered where the photos were stored from the last dive he had made earlier that year.

She moved on to another DVD—the next-to-last in the collection. There, she found his latest data and photos from February 23. The DVD contained over 4,000 high-resolution images of various plant and animal life, all taken by the deep-sea submersible's cameras.

At the end of the collection Carrie found not a photo, but instead, an illustration that seemed rather odd. It was more like a doodle than anything else. It was comprised of a hand with its pointing finger gesturing to the right, accompanied by ten words of text. The typography was highly stylized, as one might expect to find in an early 20th century newspaper advertisement. The words under the finger read simply:

You ain't seen nothin' yet. Go to DVD No. 9.

She did. And the finger was right.

Carrie popped in the next DVD, and then she clicked on the photo folder. Immediately, fifty or so thumbnails appeared. The first few images showed a mysterious bright blob. If she hadn't known better, Carrie would have thought that the photos contained artifacts from the sub's exterior lighting. She clicked on the first of the detailed images. It revealed an immense field of bluish-white light. She clicked on one of the thumbnails halfway into the photo collection. She was shocked! The camera showed a collection of—*somethings*. She thought of them as 'glowtube-tank-things'—in fact, lots of glowtube-tanks. There were far too many to count. Carrie kept clicking on images. A dozen or so later, she spotted an object from which she could judge the scale and magnitude of what she was looking at—clearly visible in the upper left corner of the photo, lying on the bottom of the ocean floor, was a close-up shot of a tank with the words *DSV SIMON-WHOI* painted along its side. She had seen photos of *Simon* on the Woods Hole Oceanographic Institute's web site before. She was reasonably certain that the object in question was one of *Simon's* eight ballast tanks. Carrie assumed that Winship must have jettisoned the tank on purpose in order to obtain an accurate scale of the objects in the photographs. She recalled the tanks on the *Simon* were about five feet in length. Winship mentioned the tank trick somewhere; there were still many audio files on the DVDs she hadn't yet listened to.

Wow!

The jettisoned tank had settled alongside two or three of the glowtube-tank-thingies. The close-up photo with the reference object clearly showed that each individual glowtube tank was approximately the same size and length as the sub's ballast tank: five feet long—give or take—and roughly six inches in diameter.

Carrie clicked back on one of the early photos in the collection, a photo showing a sizeable portion of the field. She squinted at it; she could barely discern a few of the tiny, individual glowtube tanks in this photo. Carrie did some calculations on paper. She estimated that the field covered at least a square kilometer.

God, it's bright!

Carrie tried to imagine what this oddity must have looked like to the lone, solitary scientist as he crept along in his tiny submarine, exploring this alien world at depths of 19,000 feet.

Like a scene from the movie, The Abyss*!*

Carrie wished she had the opportunity to study one of the specimens first-hand. They must be magnificent creatures.

* * *

Log entry: DSV Simon, *February 23, 1400 hours UTC. Coordinates: 1°40'N, 89°16'W—approximately 500 miles south-southeast of the Archipiélago de Colón—better known as the Galápagos Islands. Dr. Henry Winship piloting the Simon.*

At approximately 1330 hours on this date, I achieved a record depth of 19,395 feet in the Simon*. For the record, I state the following: I knowingly exceeded the recommended operational limits of this vessel by over two thousand feet. But it was necessary, in order to retrieve what are, perhaps, some of the most amazing samples of animal life—at least, I* believe *them to be animal that I— scratch that—that* anyone *has ever before witnessed.*

The items in question are cylindrical in shape, and approximately 1.75 meters long and 24 cm. in diameter. There are tens of thousands of these brightly lit objects comprising a field on the ocean floor below, covering an area of approximately 2 to 2.5 square kilometers. I do not know at this time if their photoemission is the result of bioluminescence, or chemiluminescence, or even, eletrochemiluminescence.

I was able to retrieve two of the samples in the Simon's *mechanical arm and stow them away in a side compartment. The samples are quite fragile, and in fact, I damaged them in the arm as I was retrieving them. I suspect that they may not survive the journey to the surface, given the pressure differential at sea level. But it is my hope that further, detailed analysis of the material in the samples will yield valuable data as to the nature of the samples' composition, along with the nature of their unique luminescence.*

* * *

The short con tower of the *Simon (DSV-6)* broke the surface waves, becoming visible to all those aboard its mother ship, the deep submergence support vessel *R/V Atlantis (AGOR-25)*. Inside the Simon, Dr. Henry Winship gave the hand signal through the porthole to the scuba divers to attach the main support cable. An A-frame crane on *Atlantis'* deck was set to hoist Simon out of the water and onto the deck. *Simon* was the successor to the highly successful *Alvin (DSV-2)* that made over four thousand dives since it was commissioned in 1964. *Simon* was its younger brother, commissioned in early 2011. It was equipped with an even thicker titanium pressure hull than that of the *Alvin's*—almost three inches, roughly 76 millimeters in thickness.

In one of *Simon's* storage compartments, Winship had stowed the fruits of his latest dive: two cylindrical objects he had retrieved from over 19,000 feet below on the Pacific Ocean floor. Fifteen minutes later, when *Simon* was safely stowed on *Atlantis'* deck, Winship opened the hatch and hopped out. Without so much as a greeting or acknowledgement to the other crew members, he immediately ran over to a storage closet and retrieved one of the large waterproof lockers that was kept inside. He put the locker onto a wheeled dolly and brought it over to *Simon's* aft compartment. Winship slowly twisted the door handle open. One or two curious support crew members hovered nearby to see what had captivated Winship and held his undivided attention.

Winship popped the storage door open. But instead of witnessing two long, cylindrical objects with an eerie bluish glow, Winship saw a clear, gelatinous substance oozing out of the compartment and dripping into the locker. It exhibited none of the spectacular luminescence that he had observed on the ocean's bottom.

To say that Winship was disappointed was an understatement.

* * *

"What is that stuff, Henry?"

"Damned if I know, Arthur. Damned if I know."

Dr. Arthur Cobbson of the Woods Hole Oceanographic Institution was peering over Winship's shoulder. Winship held what looked like a cooking ladle and was using it to scoop a liquid sample from the glowtube cylinders—or, more accurately, what remained of them—into a one-liter container.

"This the stuff from your last dive?"

"Yep. I tell you, Arthur, you should have seen those things! There was a field on the ocean floor comprised of tens of thousands of them. I haven't gone back through the photos yet to do an accurate estimate. The trouble is, the field is located far too deep to go there again safely."

"You took the *Simon* below its rated depth? Henry, there'll be hell to pay when they find out!"

"I know," replied Winship. "But there comes a time in a scientist's career—let me rephrase that—there comes a time in a *man's life* when he is confronted with something so major, so profound, that he'll risk everything: wealth, reputation, perhaps even his own life. This was *that* time."

"Wow," said Cobbson. "And this stuff produces some sort of photoluminescence? Or electroluminescence? And the samples—they were glowing the whole time? Even after you had harvested?"

"Not only that, Arthur—the *Simon's* instrument sensors on the arm were detecting thermal readings as well. Those animals were several degrees warmer than the ambient water temperature. The field is so warm, in fact, it supports an entire ecosystem in and around it. I saw all manner of fish and other plant life. You can imagine the implications, right?"

"Have you told anyone?" asked Cobbson.

"No, not yet. I want to nail down some preliminary findings first. Otherwise, the scientific community will label me as a crackpot."

"I hear you, Henry," Cobbson replied.

Cobbson watched silently for a few more minutes as Winship worked on the preparation of the sample. Winship made a small slide from the liquid and he slipped it under a microscope. After a few minutes, Cobbson could see that Winship was completely engrossed in his work, and oblivious to Cobbson's presence.

"I'll see you later, Henry."

Winship failed to acknowledge Cobbson's departure.

Later that afternoon, Arthur Cobbson pulled out a business card from his Rolodex. The card bore the name "Stephen R. Peterson, Vice President, Research & Development," along with an address, phone number and email. The company name on the card read in big, bold letters:

ROCKLAND GLOBAL ENERGY

In a smaller typeface, underneath, it proclaimed:

A Division of Furst AGW.

* * *

"Is this Dr. Henry Winship?"

"Yes."

"Hello, Dr. Winship. This is Steve Peterson from Rockland Global Energy. How are you today, sir?"

There was silence from Winship for a few seconds. Finally, he spoke up.

"Peters… Peterson. Hey, listen—whatever you're selling, I'm not interested. Now, goodb…"

"Wait, Dr. Winship. I'm not selling anything. In fact, I'm actually in the market to *buy* from you."

"That's interesting," said Winship. "Because I've nothing to sell."

"Ah! Perhaps you *think* you don't, Doctor. May I call you Henry? Please, call me Steve."

"If it pleases you. *Steve*. So what is it you think I have that's for sale? I'm just an old-fashioned scientific researcher who studies oceanography and takes very deep dives under the water."

"Henry, we've been following with great interest the recent discoveries you made during your dive off the Galápagos Islands this spring and…"

"How do you know about this?" demanded Winship.

"Well, Henry, good news spreads quickly. Many in the energy industry are beginning to hear about it. In fact, they can hardly wait for you to publish your initial findings."

Winship thought for a moment. It was true, he hadn't been

particularly secretive about the discovery of the glow cylinders; nor had he required those with whom he had spoken to sign a non-disclosure agreement. Winship made a mental note to go back and obtain their signatures on a generic NDA, and to backdate them to earlier in the spring.

"Just supposing for a moment that this is true—that I did make a discovery off the Galápagos earlier this year. What interest is it of your company—ah, Rockland International?"

"Rockland Global Energy, Henry. We are a huge player in the global energy market. We've recently diversified and we're now into all kinds of alternative energy programs: wind, solar, tidal—you name it. We're a $25 billion dollar company, and growing. Please don't blame any of your colleagues. We do our market research, and we recently learned about your exciting discovery of the new life forms on which you've been conducting experiments. Believe me when I say this, Henry, we could make this a very, very lucrative business transaction for you, or your Institute, or both."

"Could you guarantee me complete and total academic freedom to pursue any line of research with these creatures as I please?"

"Well, we might be able to…"

Winship cut him off in mid-sentence.

"Could you promise that any subsequent inventions would be used for the global good?"

"Henry, surely you must realize that…"

"Yeah, right. I didn't think so. Goodbye, Stevie Whatever-your-name-is."

Winship slammed down the phone. He felt unsettled, but also oddly at peace.

* * *

Udofia was making his morning trek to the village well. It was a fine day—humid and hot—in the small village of Oniuhia in Southeastern Nigeria. Udofia felt the goddess Ala was casting a radiating smile upon her people.

Nevertheless, "Udo"—as his friends and family called him—was troubled on this day. Another of the village children had taken ill. The boy had suffered bouts of diarrhea, headaches and vomiting. He was no worse, but he was no better, either. Two weeks previously, another child had suffered from a seizure. And two weeks before that, the mother of one of the sick children had begun to cough up blood. She died within hours.

The village medicine woman had applied an herbal ointment over the chest of the most recent victim. She had also chanted the customary songs to invoke the gods and goddesses to render their healing powers upon the little girl. When the child failed to respond favorably two days later, her parents, in desperation, took her to the hospital in the city of Abakaliki, 120 kilometers distant. They had promised to call the elders on the village's communal cell phone but so far no one had heard any news from them or from the hospital about the little girl's condition.

Udo couldn't help but wonder if the village people had done something to offend Ala, or her father, Chuku, "The First Great Cause." There *had* been some petty thievery recently. In response, the village elders held a series of meetings in the community to ask the guilty party to come forward and return the property and to ask the gods for forgiveness. No one had done so. The Elders were surprised; some thought that perhaps it was because the perpetrators were not from the village, and that they had traveled from one of the larger towns and cities of Mgbo, Onueke, or Ezzamgbo in the dead of night to loot the villagers' communal supplies as they slept. But no one was certain.

Udo approached the well. He saw a small congregation of villagers present. His good friend and neighbor, Esan, stood among them. He was speaking with someone Udo did not recognize. It was probably a man from the neighboring village of Ezeumo, approximately ten kilometers distant. Occasionally, they would come to draw water from Oniuhia's well on days when their water tasted bad or turned color. Unfortunately, this seemed to be occurring to the residents of Ezeumo with greater frequency.

As he got closer, Udo heard shouts that sounded like desperate pleas from the strange man. The man was gesturing to Esan, pointing at

Esan's bucket and then, at his. He seemed to be whipping himself into an emotional frenzy. Esan looked very distraught as well.

"What is it, my friends? What is troubling you so on this fine day?" Udo asked.

The stranger looked at Udo, and then at Esan. Esan appeared to be on the verge of tears. Esan tipped his bucket, allowing some of the liquid to spill onto the ground. Udo was horrified! Instead of pure, clear water, Esan's bucket ushered forth a thick, putrid, brownish substance that reeked of oil.

* * *

"These the reports?"

Dan Henderson, Manager of Rockland Global Energy's East Nigerian Operations, accepted the paperwork from his assistant manager, Hal Goldman. Standing behind his desk, he thumbed through the first couple of pages. A frown formed on Henderson's weathered face. A 30-year veteran of the oil drilling and excavation industry, Henderson knew what he was looking at meant big trouble.

"'Fraid so, Dan. Like we suspected, that last well blew out sideways."

"Damn!" Henderson said, slapping the report down on his desk. "How bad is it?"

"Pretty bad," said Goldman. "From what we can tell, we think that there's ingress into a significant portion of the Ebonyi aquifer. It happened about 2,000 feet down. This past week we've been getting scattered reports of well water contamination from as far as 120 clicks away."

Henderson sank into his chair, muttering obscenities. Then he paused. He appeared to be lost deep in thought for a minute.

"Those assholes in corporate are going to have a field day with this one. And you know what *really* burns my butt? I told 'em. *I-don't-know-how-many-times-I-told 'em* that this was inevitable with all of the short cuts they've ordered us to take. And just to save a few pennies! Now it's going to cost the company millions in cleanup costs, assuming we can even *do* anything about it."

"I know, Dan. I know." Goldman paused, and then he asked, "What *are* we going to do about it?"

"Hell if I know," replied Henderson, uncharacteristically. "Guess I'd better call New York. This is *way* beyond my pay grade now."

The next morning, Henderson sat with Goldman and six other managers of the company, in the crowded conference room of their one-story headquarters building near the company oil fields.

"Guys, I spoke at around 9 o'clock last night our time with the people in corporate. I have to tell you—what I'm about to say makes me sick. It literally makes me want to vomit. It's despicable, and it's unconscionable."

Henderson took a deep breath, exhaled, and then he continued.

"We've been ordered to cut and run."

Puzzled looks were exchanged between everyone at the table.

"What the fuck, Dan?!"

"I know. It absolutely stinks! But we're to abandon the operation and fly to New York, and a week later, to our Houston office. Corporate says that they want to debrief us, first."

"Yeah, *right*!" said one of the managers. "What they *really* mean is, 'We want you all to have your stories straight, in case the press comes knocking at your door.'"

There were more exclamations, along with shouts of obscenities from the meeting attendees. Henderson gestured with his hands for quiet.

"You're probably right. But tomorrow, we'll all going to board a chartered flight from Abakaliki to Lagos; from there, we go to Heathrow, and then on to JFK. In the meantime, we've been instructed not to discuss any of this with the locals; and not even with our friends and family back in the States."

"So, corporate wants us to abandon three rigs valued at fifty million dollars apiece?" asked one of the managers. "We just stick our thumbs up our asses and pretend like we were never here?"

"If you want your next paycheck, then, yes—that's *exactly* what they expect you to do," replied Henderson. "Like I said, it *absolutely stinks*."

As the meeting drew to a close, Henderson spoke quietly to the assembled men.

"I want to thank you for your service to Rockland, gentlemen. When we get to New York, I am tendering my resignation, effective immediately."

There was a hush over the room, followed by a sudden outpouring: "Don't let the bastards win, Dan!" "Good luck, Dan." "Give 'em hell."

Henderson motioned for silence again.

"I don't know if any of you are men of God. But, I ask our heavenly Father to forgive us for what we've done to this country. I especially ask that He look out after all of the poor souls in this region whose only source of drinking water we've just poisoned."

"Amen."

CHAPTER TEN

Terrance and Edward Smith-Hughes had lived together in the triple-decker apartment house a few blocks off Massachusetts Avenue in Cambridge for six years. Before the two met, it had been Terrance's home for fifteen years prior. Terrance liked the relatively quiet neighborhood situated only a few blocks from the hustle and bustle of Cambridge's Central Square. The T-stop was an easy walk from their front door. Thus, the location was ideal for his commute to the East Cambridge Neighborhood Health Center where Terrance served as the Director of Mental Health Services as well as the sole practicing mental health clinician on the staff. While his fancy title could not completely offset the sting of his ridiculously low salary (coupled with no raises for the past five years), Terrance truly loved the interaction he had with members of the community—most of whom lived near or below the official poverty level.

Terrance's clientele were primarily lower income women and children of Portuguese heritage with a mix of Irish and Italian. Many were, unfortunately, teenage mothers of small children born out of wedlock. Terrance felt badly for these girls. They were far too young to be shouldering such a huge responsibility. Counseling and birth control, along with STD screening, comprised a huge portion of the clinic's daily workload.

During his tenure at the clinic, Terrance had seen a marked

change in attitudes in this insular community toward race, religion, and even sexual orientation. He recalled a time when he had found it necessary to remain "closeted" even to his fellow employees at the clinic. Just a few years ago, a gay lifestyle in the Portuguese community would not have been tolerated. Things were much better now, both for the residents of East Cambridge as well as the people who served them. Terrance no longer had to hide his sexual preference if it happened to come up in conversation. Even so, a few remaining holdout grandmothers and older men had made it clear to the clinic's Executive Director that they would not allow their children to enter into counseling sessions with the "queer" doctor.

* * *

Terrance Smith was raised as an only child in a middle-class family in Syracuse, New York, to a loving mother and father. He knew at an early age that he was "different" although it would have been presumptuous to assign the word "gay" or "homosexual" to that feeling at the time. Later, during the time in a boy's life when the first stirrings of desire and curiosity about sex begin to bloom, Terrance felt those stirrings, too. But, he was deeply ashamed of his feelings, for his fantasies and desires were for boys. Society had awful names for people who felt those sorts of feelings. His so-called friends were cruel with their name-calling and ridicule for Terrance. Consequently, Terrance retreated deep into the closet. It lasted well into his college years.

Since Edward had come into his life, however, every day felt like a blessing for Terrance. Instead of simply helping others to try to live happier lives, Terrance could truly say that he, too, felt alive and happy. Even on bad days, Terrance marveled at being able to appreciate some small facet of his existence, however mundane: a tiny flower growing in the crack of the sidewalk; a sunny day; or a smile from a stranger.

Terrance found his career in psychotherapy to be immensely satisfying. And he felt a deep love for his life-partner, Edward. Terrance had also grown to appreciate the close relationship he enjoyed with his best friend, Carrie Bloomfield. When Carrie moved into the upstairs apartment seven years earlier, it was as though Terrance gained the older sister he never had. He and Carrie had taken an instant liking to one another. Carrie was one of the most kind and gentle people he knew. He marveled at how Carrie had coped with her traumatic, life-changing decision to undergo elective, bilateral mastectomy surgery at the age of forty-one—with little or no emotional support from family or friends.

It must have been devastating for her!

After their friendship had solidified, Carrie showed Terrance the beautiful tattoo that adorned her chest, and that skillfully covered up scar tissue. He was very impressed. Terrance told Carrie that he had once gotten his nipples pierced, but soon abandoned the piercings because they were too uncomfortable when they rubbed against his clothes.

Carrie had gradually opened up to Terrance about her family, too, and the history of mental illness on her mother's side. Terrence was somewhat surprised to hear Carrie's self-deprecating assessment of her intellectual gifts. She downplayed them, attributing her intelligence solely to genetic probabilities. It seemed that Carrie's humility allowed her little room for self-admiration. Terrance had read various papers in the scientific literature that concluded there were links between intellectual giftedness and bipolar disorder. Terrance, however, was certain that Carrie exhibited none of the classic symptoms of the disease.

He perceived that his gifted scientist-girlfriend was not only humble about her intellectual prowess but that she also downplayed her successes in business. Although she had never spoken openly about it, Terrance suspected that Carrie was a wealthy woman. He had once seen a letter on Carrie's kitchen table from a local women's shelter addressed to the SEB Foundation. The letter in her possession had been sent to a post office box address with a downtown Boston zip code. He hadn't wanted to be nosy, but something about the name "SEB Foundation" caught his attention. Then, it clicked: Terrance recalled that a foundation with that same name had made a sizeable donation to his employer, the East Cambridge Neighborhood Health Center, two years previous. It seemed too much to be simply coincidental. He wondered, too, if there was possibly a connection between the name "SEB" and the initials of Carrie's deceased sister, Samantha Elizabeth Bloomfield.

* * *

"Thanks for letting me hang out with you guys tonight. I was feeling a little lonely," Carrie said to Terrance as she came in the front door to their apartment on a Friday night.

Edward came up and gave Carrie a hug and said, "Tell us the truth, now—it wouldn't happen to have *anything* to do with a certain *someone* being out of town, would it?"

Carrie's new boyfriend, Paul Santiago, had driven back to New Jersey earlier that afternoon to visit his family. He was scheduled to return to Boston late Sunday night.

"Well…maybe." Carrie smiled. She and Paul had gone on a couple of dates. She'd be lying if she told them she didn't feel just a slight bit of attraction for the fascinating young painter who was studying at the Massachusetts College of Art and Design.

Carrie changed the subject.

"Here are a couple of nice Cabernet Sauvignons. Or, so I was told by the guy at Liquor World."

She handed the bottles over to Terrance. He made a big show out of inspecting the labels.

"Oh, yes. Mm-hum. 2009—a *very* good year." He snickered. In response, Carrie swatted his shoulder, and said, "Stop it! You know I don't drink that much. What do *I* know about wine?"

"I'm sorry," said Terrance. "We know that you have other—shall we say—'stronger suits.'"

"I bet you're a cheap date, Carrie Bloomfield," chimed in Edward.

"*You'll* never know, will you?" quipped Carrie.

She reached into her backpack.

"I didn't know what you guys had for entertainment. I have with me…Ta-da!"

Carrie held out a copy of *The Adventures of Buckaroo Banzai Across the Eighth Dimension.* Then, she pulled out two more DVDs, each containing *Outer Limits* episodes. One was entitled, *Don't Open Till Doomsday*; the other, *The Premonition.*

"Ooh, ooh!" exclaimed Edward. "*Don't Open Till Doomsday.* A classic! Season One, Episode Seventeen."

"You certainly know your *Outer Limits*, don't you," she remarked.

"And his inner limits, too," said Terrance. "Speaking of which, my tummy says time for Chinese takeout. Quick! What are we having?"

* * *

The trio made strong inroads into several containers variously filled with mushi pork, vegetarian delight, General Tso's chicken, and hot and sour soup, after which they retired to the living room. Edward opened the second bottle of wine. He topped off Terrance and Carrie's glasses. Their conversation turned to dating and romantic involvements.

"Terrance was an awful slut before I met him," said Edward.

"Yes, I slept with every *one* and every *thing*," Terrance laughed. "I even slept with a woman once."

"Really!" Edward replied, with mock surprise. "You never told me this, honey. How was it?"

"Yes, do tell!" chimed in Carrie.

"It was okay," replied Terrance. "She was a nice girl. This was in the mid-eighties, during a time in my life when I was trying to convince myself that I could be straight if I really wanted to. We dated for a couple of months. I think she knew that my heart wasn't really in it, though."

"You mean your genitals, dear."

"Yes, that too." Terrance paused to take a sip of wine. "After we broke up, I went on a holy tear. I would pick up a different guy at the gay bars almost every night. That phase lasted well over a year."

"You're lucky you didn't pick up anything else," remarked Carrie.

"Oh, I was extra careful. AIDS, well, actually GRID—you know, Gay-Related Immune Deficiency—had just made its debut into the gay community." Terrance appeared thoughtful for a moment. He added, "It claimed a lot of my friends."

"I'm sorry," replied Carrie.

Carrie shared with them the story about her first love, Jim, and how he had taken advantage of her during their first year when both were working on their doctorates in O'Connor's lab.

"That's *awful*, dear!" remarked Edward. "What an uncivilized brute. *Shame* on him!"

"Yes. He certainly had no business being in science. But the sex was wonderful."

They laughed.

Upon hearing the trio's laughter, Fee-fee—Edward and Terrance's little poodle—started to bark.

"Hush, Fee-fee!" Terrance scolded her.

Carrie continued by telling them about a handful of one-night stands she had had over the years. After more light banter, Carrie announced to them, shyly, "I made out with a girl, once."

The two gay men immediately stared at her; their shocked expressions transformed into huge grins that could have been mistaken for those of two Cheshire cats.

Finally, Edward responded. He said, slowly, "Do tell!"

"Well, there isn't much to tell. We struck up a conversation at the Plough & Stars one night. She was a writer. I was fascinated to hear about how she researched her subjects and gathered information about all of the places and people..."

"Tell us about the *sex*!"

"Hush, Edward. She's getting to it! It's *her* story—let *her* tell it."

"Thank you, Terrance." Carrie continued. "Anyway, I was enjoying listening to her describe all the preparation she put into writing a novel. It reminded me of all the steps one takes in preparing a scientific experiment. It was a very noisy bar and so I was sitting quite close to her so that I could hear her. She paused for a second, and then I looked up at her. Our faces were only inches apart. I was looking into her eyes, and the next..."

"Yes, yes!"

"Well, before I knew it, she leaned over and kissed me right on the mouth. I was shocked! But I didn't pull away. It was one of the most tender, loving kisses I'd ever received."

"Any tongue action?"

Carrie shot Edward a dirty look. She continued.

"We kissed a couple of more times at the bar, and then we went outside to her car and we made out—and before you ask me—no, there wasn't any action below the belt. We both kept our clothes on."

"What happened then?"

"Nothing. She and I were feeling around, and she made the discovery about my chest. I explained to her what had happened. She said that she was okay with it, that it didn't make her uncomfortable."

Carrie took another sip of wine, and then she continued with her story.

"She asked me if I wanted to go home with her, but by then I guess I was starting to chicken out. Kissing and touching is one thing, but going further than that—well, I think it would have weirded me out. Don't get me wrong, I think I was actually attracted to her, and a part of me really *wanted* to go home with her. But the idea of 'doing it' with another woman just didn't feel right."

Carrie took the last sip of her wine, and smiled sadly. Then she said quietly, almost to herself, "Funny, isn't it? Here was this person who was willing to overlook my severe deformities and make a connection with me, but I wasn't open-minded enough to reciprocate. I was too worried about what society calls 'normal.'"

* * *

A little later, Terrance, Edward and Carrie settled in together on the couch with Fee-fee to watch *Don't Open Till Doomsday*. Edward kept up a running commentary throughout the flick. They both told him to shut up so that they could hear the actual dialogue. Afterwards, the three chatted some more. Carrie asked Terrance about his work.

"It breaks my heart to see some of these young girls at the clinic who come in pregnant. They hold such potential! But they've been so engrained with those Catholic beliefs. They think that they must do right by God and the Church. Most of them feel trapped into having the baby. Abortion isn't an option."

Terrance continued.

"Then, of course, they drop out of school, promising they'll go for their GEDs after they give birth. But—and I've seen this *so* many times—they commit to putting the baby up for adoption, only to have some well-meaning parent or family member talk them out of it. Alas, they become one in a long line of unwed mothers, perpetuating the downward spiral into poverty."

Carrie grimaced, and shook her head. She, too, thought it was a shame.

"For what it's worth, I volunteer to talk to girls in the local Cambridge public school system about math and science," Carrie said. "But I don't know if my message gets through to them."

"You have such a good heart, my dear." Terrance reached over and patted Carrie on the shoulder.

"Ooh! Group hug! Group hug!" shouted Edward.

Eventually, their talk turned to Carrie's work. Without going into a lot of detail about the death of Winship and the sinister Furst AGW, Carrie described to Edward and Terrance her efforts to develop a promising compound that could lead to new forms of alternative energy.

"I've had a few setbacks in the lab, but essentially the research is proceeding at an amazing clip. The cellular metabolism in this 'worm juice' is unlike anything I've ever seen, or, for that matter, *anyone* has ever seen. These cells seem to comprise a little bit of plant and a little bit of animal. When all is said and done, I wouldn't be at all surprised if the scientific community defines a completely new biological classification for these magnificent life forms."

She continued.

"When light hits them, the rate of energy conversion and output is roughly ten-fold over what one might expect to achieve with today's best solar panel technology. And that's even before applying some optimization steps that I'm working on."

"Don't you have to go back to the bottom of the ocean and harvest more of these worms for it to be practical, dear?" asked Edward.

"Perhaps, eventually. But for now, just using the existing sample that contains a small number of still-living cells that Winship kept for me

I've been able to reproduce sizeable quantities of the stuff in a lab environment. It's like home brewing beer on a small scale—except it's a lot trickier and it doesn't smell as bad. In fact, there's no odor at all."

"Wow," remarked Terrance. "This sounds very revolutionary. It's far outside of your normal area of expertise, isn't it?"

"Terrance, now you *know* our Carrie is a genius. Nothing is outside her expertise."

"Gosh—thanks, Edward. I love you, too. But I'm afraid all of those rumors that I walk on water are greatly exaggerated. And yes, Terrance, it's far, far outside of my area of expertise, which is in the design and implementation of biological diagnostics and medical devices."

Terrance appeared pensive. He said, "If this succeeds, your new technology will be perceived as a significant threat to the established energy industry. Did you ever stop to think that the research you're doing right now *might* lead to the birth of an entirely new oligopoly?"

Carrie looked at Terrance. Her face took on a distressed expression. She didn't immediately answer him. In seconds, the mood in the room had transformed from excited enthusiasm into something that seemed quite serious. Terrance wished he hadn't opened this can of worms.

"Hey—I kid! I kid! So the world will have a better solar panel, right?" He forced a grin. Edward grinned, too. After a second or two, Carrie smiled, weakly. But her disposition was markedly more somber for the remainder of the evening.

* * *

Mary Cadwell Bloomfield grew up in Racine, Wisconsin, the youngest of three girls. Mary's last memory of her father, John Cadwell was of his waving goodbye to her and her mother, Madeline, as he boarded the train in Milwaukee to go off to war. She was eight years old. Madeline kept the home fires burning for John for well over five years, until all hope of her husband returning was exhausted. Mary's father was legally declared dead in 1947, one among thousands of servicemen who were never accounted for in the World War II Pacific Theater.

According to Carrie's grandma, Mary was "smart as a whip" but she was also a "terribly difficult child," much like her older sister Emma. Mary could be moody for days on end and then, suddenly she would "snap out of it" and be "as gay as a sunflower." Mary had few friends in school, no doubt because she was prone to saying the most awful things about them. She would be penitent, of course, but by then the damage had been done. Many a young man of her age had labeled Mary as spoiled, immature and cruel. But young Richard Bloomfield didn't think so. After a brief courtship, he was smitten; he fell head over heels for the fair, red-haired lass from Racine. In his eyes, she could do no wrong— even when she *was* being mean and pig-headed. He proposed to her in the spring of 1954; they married in October of that year. Their first bundle of joy came almost nine months to the day after their wedding. She was named Samantha Elizabeth Bloomfield. In the years that followed, they had another girl, Carrie Elizabeth, followed by two sons, William and Earl.

Carrie recalled her father telling her that Carrie's mother flew into a rage upon learning of his plans to name their second daughter Caroline. John thought that Caroline was a beautiful name. It had been his mother's middle name, and used by women in his family for generations.

"No, not Caroline! No daughter of mine will be named Caroline. It's a hideous name! End of discussion."

After Mary calmed down somewhat, she surprised her husband and offered him a compromise. "Carrie would be okay, I guess."

John happily agreed to name his daughter Carrie—short for Caroline. It was perhaps one of the last times in their marriage that Mary would compromise on anything.

* * *

When faced with the daunting task of deciding upon elective mastectomy surgery, Carrie had started compiling an extensive family medical history. Fortunately for Carrie, her aunt Emma was a prolific genealogist and scrapbooking enthusiast. Armed with Emma's records, which included medical histories and anecdotal stories about other family members, Carrie started to see a clear pattern emerge. Women in her family had been hospitalized on numerous occasions; there were frequent stays in the local sanatorium for "mental exhaustion and fatigue" along with recurring mood swings and temper tantrums. Most of these individuals were credited with having superior intelligence. In Carrie's mind, it confirmed the psychosis coined by the German psychiatrist Emil Kraeplin in the late nineteen century: manic-depressive behavior, referred to nowadays as bipolar disorder.

Carrie feared at times that she, too, might be borderline bipolar. She was finally comforted by a psychiatrist friend who informed her about symptoms to be on guard for and then said, simply, "After all, Carrie, if you aren't loose around the edges by your age now, it's unlikely you ever will be. But think of your mind as having the potential—for good or ill—of a race car, not a sedan. So it will be a good thing if you never experiment with psychotropic substances."

CHAPTER ELEVEN

To a casual observer, the large Siamese cat appeared as though it was suffering an epileptic seizure. It was a rather scary sight: Samantha's eyelids vibrated rapidly, and then her eyes started to roll to and fro. Next, her tail began to twitch, and then her body began making the same motions or movements. One could also hear a soft sucking noise emanating from her mouth. Fortunately, though, this wasn't one of Sam's nine lives being snuffed out. The cat was merely in a deep REM sleep.

The hunter burst through the thicket, surprising her prey. Just ahead, the brownish-grey tree rat with its bushy tail zigzagged and gyrated wildly in a desperate attempt to throw off its pursuer. It could not elude Samantha that easily, however. Sam stayed glued to the rat's twitching tail, locking in on it like a laser. It was frustrating! A few times she almost had the rat. Still, though, it was just a matter of time before the rat tired and she could close the gap, and sink her claws into the...

"MEEEEOOOOOOWWWWW!!!"

"Oh, shit! Sorry, cat." Paul quickly rolled back in the opposite direction after inadvertently smothering the sleeping Sam who had been nestled between him and Carrie. Sam did not understand why her mistress allowed this rude human male to intrude upon their sanctum. She wasted no time hopping off the bed, and, in the process, bouncing claws-first off Carrie's back.

"Ow!" cried Carrie. She sighed.

"Good one, Paul," she said, in a low, monotone voice that made clear her irritation.

"I'm sorry, Carrie. You heard me apologize to Samantha, right? It's just that, well, I'm not used to sharing a bed with an animal, okay?"

As he spoke, Carrie rolled over onto her back. Paul gently touched his finger to Carrie's chest. His fingers traced along the outline of the large, multi-colored tattoo that adorned her body: a muscular genie with flashing eyes, one ear pierced with a large gold hoop. The genie sported a dark beard and mustache; his head was topped with an elaborate turban. The upper half of the genie's body rose out of an intricately decorated bottle, his arms outstretched. In the palm of each hand, the genie held a bird's nest. One nest contained a white dove; the other, a Peregrine falcon. The artist was nationally known—a woman who practiced out of a small shop in Seabrook, New Hampshire. She had done an amazing job with the piece, thought Carrie. The artwork hid most of the scarring from the mastectomy performed twelve years earlier.

"I dig your body," Paul said. He kissed her mouth tenderly.

"*You* just dig my *art*."

"No, I don't. I dig *you*. *All* of you."

"Well, just don't dig me *too* much. You remember the understanding we have? We're—Just—Good—Friends—Okay?" With each word, she stabbed his chest with her finger for added emphasis.

Paul sighed. He returned her gaze, and then he gave a small affirmative nod. An awkward moment passed between them.

"Paul," Carrie began. "We've not actually had a serious conversation about it. How do you really feel about—this?" She took his hand and pressed it against her chest—first on the left side, and then on the right—where once there had been breasts and nipples. "You know. My not having 'boobs' anymore. It must make you feel a *little* uncomfortable, right?"

He paused, and then smiled.

"Does not."

"Does, too," she shot back.

"Does not."

She giggled. "Does, too."

"Does not."

"Does, too—Ahhhhhhhh!"

Carried cried out, playfully, as Paul grabbed for her armpits and began to tickle her.

"UNCLE! UNCLE!"

"Hey, I want to paint you in the nude sometime. Would that be okay?"

"No way, José," replied Carrie. "Do you think I have the luxury of time to sit in a chair all day in my birthday suit while you do your thing? I barely get done what I need to do. Besides, don't all of you fledging artists use pretty co-eds from the university for your nude modeling?"

"I don't want to paint *them*. I want to paint *you*. Warts, scars, genies, and all."

* * *

Carrie arrived home to her apartment after a full day of experiments at the Whitehead Institute. She slipped the key into the lock of her front door and turned it.

That's odd!

The lock offered no resistance; it was already open. Had she forgotten to lock up behind her this morning? Paul had access to her spare key, but he wouldn't have let himself in without first calling her.

She entered, tentatively, calling out, "Hello?" As she wheeled in her bike, she stopped to survey her surroundings. She received a terrible shock.

The place had been ransacked!

Drawers had been pulled from cabinets and upended. Silverware and cookbooks were strewn across the floor. Pictures were removed from the walls. Their backs had been torn off. Carrie got an even bigger shock when she entered the bedroom. Clothes were scattered everywhere. The bed's mattress was sitting on its box springs at an odd angle. Her Dell computer had been partly disassembled. Its case was sitting on the bed; the chassis was on the floor. It was missing its hard disk. She scanned the surface of her desk. All of her diaries were missing, and her personal USB jump drives were gone, too.

Suddenly, Carrie felt something brush up against her leg. She looked down, and saw Samantha Elizabeth Bloomfield, II, standing next to her. The cat looked only too happy to see her owner.

Thank God you're okay, Sam!

Carrie reached down and picked up the Siamese cat. She hugged and kissed her.

"What in the hell happened here, Sam? Huh?"

* * *

Edward Hughes, Jr., was raised in a very loving home by non-traditional parents, Edward Sr. and Edna Hughes of Bakersfield, California. Like Terrance, Edward, too, was an only child, and—from his earliest memories—had felt "different" from other children. This made no difference to his father and mother. They encouraged young Edward to talk about his feelings, without being judgmental. A home-schooled child, young Edward was sheltered from many of the cruel taunts and bullying that so many gay children like Terrance had to endure. Edward Sr. was a certified horticulturist and professional landscaper. He consulted frequently on large projects, as well as for wealthy clients. His wife, Edna, was a former schoolteacher turned stay-at-home mom. They lived comfortably in a middle-class neighborhood in Bakersfield.

When it was time to spread his wings and leave the nest, Edward chose the rustic campus of Pennsylvania State University in College Park where he majored in philosophy. But his true love was for sculpture and art. Edward went on to earn his Master's degree in the Visual Arts at the City University of New York. Later, with the aid of a loan from his parents, Edward opened a small but thriving gallery on Newbury Street in Boston. He had fallen for the man of his dreams one night when the two met at a charity benefit on the South End in 2003. Theirs was an intense courtship which lasted for three months, after which time Edward moved in with Terrance in his two-bedroom, 1200 square foot apartment near

Prospect Street in Central Square. He and Terrance were wed on May 17, 2004—the first day that gay marriage was legalized in the Commonwealth of Massachusetts. They also chose to legally change their last names to *Smith-Hughes.*

Upon entering into a relationship with Terrance, Edward became the proud co-parent of a white toy poodle by the name of Fee-fee. Edward also "adopted" Terrance's best friend and "big sister"—the charming woman who lived upstairs, Carrie Bloomfield.

* * *

Apart from all her scientific achievements, Carrie Bloomfield was an active, but anonymous philanthropist in the Boston community. Numerous worthwhile organizations had benefited from her generosity. Through her SEB Foundation, Carrie had anonymously donated millions of dollars to battered women's shelters, food banks, mental health centers, and youth programs. Carrie founded the organization in 2006 to honor the memory of her deceased sister, Samantha Elizabeth Bloomfield.

Jake Shapiro served as President, Secretary, and Treasurer of the foundation; he was also its public face. On rare occasions, Carrie might accompany Jake to a reception or banquet, where he would preside over the formal presentation of an SEB gift. She would attend simply as "a good friend of Mr. Shapiro."

On the day that the SEB Foundation was formally incorporated, Carrie and Jake sat in his Beacon Hill condo to sign the official documents. The paperwork was spread out before them on Jake's living room table. It required Carrie's signature and initials on every page.

"Carrie, I know you want to retain your anonymity. But we can't easily say your sister's name in public and expect you to remain out of the limelight. What shall we say the acronym stands for?"

Carrie paused from her signing, and thought.

"You're right. I hadn't even considered that. Hmm…let me think. Shelter…Save…Seize…Seize Every…Every what?"

"I don't know," replied Jake, shrugging his shoulders.

"I'm drawing a blank for the moment."

"Well, I'll tell you what—you just keep signing your initials on every page, and I'll pour us both a glass of wine. Perhaps some spirits will help clear the blockage."

"That sounds like a capital idea, Jake," Carrie said. She returned her attention to the paperwork.

"Jesus! How many pages do I have to initial? You'd think I was taking out a mortgage or something."

Carrie had seen firsthand the fruits of her labor. She liked to ride by the new playground constructed two years ago in the schoolyard of an elementary school in West Somerville, to watch the young children play on the swing sets and the jungle gym. The squeals of delight from the boys and girls were all the confirmation Carrie needed that it had been money well spent.

On another occasion, she visited a youth center in Dorchester during the late afternoon to watch as high school kids played supervised indoor sports with their brand new athletic equipment. And one of the food banks in Cambridgeport that received regular grants from SEB also received her personal attention, when she volunteered in its kitchen.

For the East Cambridge Neighborhood Health Center, Carrie's charity had made all the difference. Although Terrance was reasonably certain that Carrie's Foundation was the source of the gift, he hadn't inquired. What he didn't know, however, was that the Health Center had only four to six months of operating capital left, after which time it would have been forced to close. Carrie had certainly saved Terrance's job, along with those of a dozen other employees.

"Let's go back to Shelter…'Shelter Every…Shelter Every *What*, though?"

"Brother?" volunteered Jake.

"No. I want to stay gender-neutral, if possible."

"'Save Every…' How about 'Save Every Breath?'"

They both shook their heads no, and laughed simultaneously.

"Sounds too much like, Save Your Breath. Hey, wait—maybe you're on to something, here, Jake. How about…Share Every Breath?"

"I *like* that."

"I do, too!" said Carrie. "Those words are also part of a song I really like, 'Need To Be Next To You' by Michelle Branch."

Carrie walked over to Jake, and said, "Thank you, kind sir!" She startled the lawyer by giving him a big hug.

CHAPTER TWELVE

There was an early December chill in the air that evening. Carrie pedaled her bike up Magazine Street towards Central Square. The trees had shed large portions of their foliage, thanks in no small measure to an unusual Halloween Nor'easter that had brought with it high winds and snow to the entire eastern seaboard. The leaves covered the pavement thickly, making it treacherous for her to navigate in spots.

Carrie was feeling a little tired. She had been stressed out from the break-in at her apartment the previous week. But Carrie had thrown herself into her work. The distraction had been a good thing. Plus, the results of her most recent experiments had been, by and large, very positive. Carrie had worked almost non-stop for the past forty-eight hours, interpreting experimental results and refining her plans on some follow up experiments. Like everything else in science, occasionally you were blessed with the opportunity to take two giant steps forward—followed by a step back. Today was a "one-step-back" day. Carrie wasn't too upset, however. This was to be expected. It was simply the nature of scientific research and discovery.

Carrie thought that she might unwind a bit by taking in a live performance that evening at the Cantab Lounge on Mass Avenue. A friend of hers was a member of an eclectic rock group who were the opening act for a more popular band. Carrie knew the drummer well. They chatted frequently about the local music scene. By day, Billy masqueraded as a mild-mannered janitor on the housekeeping staff at the Whitehead. But by night, Billy and his other middle-aged buddies donned colorful, 60s apparel and transformed themselves into the "Tsunami of Sound." Their genre was surf-rock instrumental; ToS had a unique sound—and a growing following, too, judging by the increasing number of "Likes" on their Faceboo… Carrie was jarred suddenly out of her thoughts by the sound of a rapidly accelerating vehicle that was overtaking her from behind. She instinctively jumped the curb and rode partway up into someone's front yard before turning around to take a look. A dark van with tinted windows arrived where her bike had been an instant earlier. Its tires slammed into the side of the curb with great force, and then the van bounced back into the street. Without pausing, the vehicle and its driver quickly sped away.

"Fuck me!" She exclaimed to herself.

That was close.

Carrie tried to see the license number, but the bulb that was supposed to illuminate the plate was apparently burned out.

Carrie stopped to take a few deep breaths and to calm down. Perhaps she'd skip the performance, and go straight home.

Were they trying *to hit me?*

* * *

"I don't know, Jake. First, my place gets broken into and ransacked. Then, the car incident last week. It's a little unnerving. Do you think that this has to do with Henry Winship? Is someone after the technology?"

Carrie was meeting with Jake Shapiro in Grendel's Den in Harvard Square. They found a small table next to the fireplace and started with drinks. The popping of the burning logs made for a relaxing atmosphere on the heels of yet another hectic week.

"It's possible, Carrie."

Jake paused for a moment to think.

"If it's alright, I think I'd like to assign some protection for you."

"Aw, no! I don't have time for a baby-sitter…"

"You won't have to do anything, Carrie. It'll just be two guys from an agency we use. They'll keep an eye on you discreetly, from a distance. I'll give you their names and photos, so you won't worry if you spot them hanging around. We'll give it a couple of weeks, okay?"

Carrie took a sip from her hot apple cider and rum, mulling over Jake's request.

"Well, if they stay out of my way and don't intrude…I suppose. Okay."

The waitress arrived to take their food order. Jake recommended to Carrie the hummus and pita appetizer. He explained that all the food specials were half-price during happy hour.

"Say," Carrie asked, "How'd you come to choose this venue? I didn't know that you liked to hang out in these sorts of places."

"This place? Why, hell! This is Mecca for lawyers. In fact, it used to be *the* hangout for the law school crowd. I'd come here all the time in the 90s with the interns and associates from our firm. Nowadays it's more gentrified."

"Did you know," Jake continued, "that Grendel's was ground zero for a landmark Supreme Court decision?"

"Supreme as in Massachusetts? Or U.S.?"

"U.S. of A," Jake replied. "I shit you not."

He explained.

"There was an Armenian Orthodox Church that used to sit next door, where Peet's Coffee is today. Back then, Commonwealth law said you couldn't obtain a liquor license for an establishment within 500 feet of a church without the church's express permission. In this particular situation, the church was located a mere ten feet away! Believe me, they were definitely *not* interested in seeing Grendel's serving up booze."

Jake continued, "The owner of Grendel's sued in court. Grendel's lost the decision, and they appealed to the Commonwealth's Supreme Judicial Court. The Commonwealth ruled against them. Luckily for this place, one of Grendel's most loyal patrons was a certain Harvard Law School professor by the name of Lawrence Tribe."

"I know that name," said Carrie.

"I'm not surprised. He used to get interviewed all the time on

National Public Radio. Larry took the case *pro bono* and argued it in front of the U.S. Supreme Court. Chief Justice Warren Burger wrote the majority opinion, as I recall. The Court ruled that the Massachusetts law violated the 'Lemon test' in that it 'advanced religious interests and created excessive entanglement between religion and the state.'"

"Anyway," Jake concluded, "today that church is gone. And as you can see, Grendel's is still very much here and serving up its unique brews, thanks in no small measure to Tribe's efforts. Still—I *really* wish they would add Budweiser to their menu someday."

Jake raised his Black and Tan in a toast. He clicked his glass to Carrie's and proclaimed, "*Basta!* Here's to Larry Tribe and those like him."

* * *

Carrie's research into the complex compounds extracted from living cells from the Tubeworm cylinders took her down numerous paths, which, initially, also led her into numerous dead ends.

I could spend my whole life studying this and never discover its secrets! She brooded.

But after only a few weeks of experimental work and many hunches inspired by creative dreams, Carrie's efforts were rewarded with some surprisingly successful initial findings.

Energy in a living thing is derived from a series of chemical reactions. In plants, photosynthesis is the mechanism by which the sun's energy is converted into chemical energy that fuels them. The leaves of plants contain special structures to capture sunlight, much like a solar panel. These living solar panels consist of an arrangement of chlorophyll pigments contained in its leaves, allowing the absorption and transformation of sunrays into the chemical energy. And when combined with the intake of raw materials—namely carbon dioxide and water—one observes the familiar scientific axiom: six molecules of carbon dioxide plus six molecules of water in the presence of sunlight yields one molecule of glucose.

From the start, however, Dr. Winship's creatures seemingly

played under a different set of physical rules. After the course of a series of experiments, she immediately began observing unusual behavior in the substance's Adenosine triphosphate transport chains. Further analysis revealed that the chains were amplified, producing unusually long, complex sugars. The end result was a simple, super efficient way of moving energy. It appeared to Carrie that the system suffered almost no loss. In fact, it seemed to *amplify* energy. It was analogous to the idea of inventing a sort of "super battery" in combination with a solid-state amplifier. Under conditions of extreme pressure and absence of sunlight at the bottom of the sea, the battery functioned nominally, allowing the tubeworms to give off low levels of light and energy in the form of heat. But, at normal pressure, coupled with exposure to ambient temperature and light in a lab environment, the substance behaved as though it was on steroids.

Very tiny samples of the worm juice exposed to an open environment in saline H_2O would light up and start to emit energy at an incredible rate. Carrie began to think that sufficient quantities of the material might render solar panels obsolete.

While Carrie did not pretend to understand all of the science completely, the implications of the worm juice for changing the future course of energy production were very much evident.

* * *

Three weeks after her dinner with Jake, Carrie received a call at her Nexus virtual voice mailbox number.

"Hello, Dr. Bloomfield, this is Andrew Gephardt. I'm with an executive search boutique called Premiere Leadership Services. We're based in Manhattan but we do placements nationwide. We have an exciting opportunity for someone with credentials like yours. It's a small startup playing in the alternative energy sector, and it's located inside of Route 128. The company is just beginning to court VC funding, and it needs a stellar Chief Scientific Officer. You come highly recommended. Please give me a call at your convenience so that we might discuss this opportunity. I can be reached at..."

Yeah right. Why is this particular opportunity becoming available right now? More importantly, why me? I'm not known to anyone in the alternative energy industry. Curious indeed.

Carrie grabbed another cup of coffee, and then she finished a report due later that day. Three hours later, she decided to call the number.

"Ah, Dr. Bloomfield! Thank you so much for returning my call."

"You're welcome, Dr. Gephardt."

"Please. It's just Mister. But call me Andy."

"Okay…Mr. Gephardt. So, why might you be calling *me*? I *do* have an amateur interest in the field, but surely you must know that my and Nexus Sciences' strengths lie in the life sciences, not alternative energy."

"Doctor…ah, may I call you Carrie? Carrie, my client is looking for an outside-the-box thinker—someone who is scientifically familiar with non-traditional R&D, who would thrive in a challenging, multi-disciplinary environment as a natural leader. This describes you, correct?"

"Good day, Mr. Gephardt."

"Wait…" he said. "If I may be direct, Dr. Bloomfield." The voice on the other end dropped any pretense of a sales pitch and took on a more sinister tone.

"We've learned that you've recently come into possession of materials from Dr. Winship."

Whoa. The man doesn't beat around the bush.

"That's an interesting piece of intelligence there, Mr. Gephardt. I hope you didn't have to pay for it, because I'm afraid you're barking up the wrong tree. I vaguely recall having met a Dr. Winship once—at Woods Hole, I believe. But I haven't the foggiest idea about any materials. With regard to the CSO position, I'd be happy to refer you to a very talented individual here in the greater Boston area who possesses the qualities you're seeking, and *does* work in that sector. Now, I'm afraid I'm very busy at the moment. Goodbye, Mr. Gephardt."

* * *

"So, who are these creeps, Jake?"

Carrie and Jake were having margaritas at The Border Café on Church Street in Harvard Square. The noise level inside had been rising steadily since their arrival several hours earlier. The number of patrons was also steadily increasing. The noise was actually a welcome thing for both Carrie and Jake. Jake, too, was beginning to feel a little paranoid about possible eavesdropping, after hearing of the headhunting call to Carrie from Premiere earlier in the week.

"I had our people do a little digging into this group. They're legitimate, all right. They do several million in revenue annually placing scientific executives. A shell company owns Premiere. And another owns it. And another. And another. And so on, and so on. There are *eight* levels of shell companies in all—until we finally get to the top. You ready for this? It's Furst AGW."

"No way!"

"Yes," replied Jake. "You heard me right."

Jake took another sip from his glass.

"I had a nasty encounter with them in the First Circuit Appeals Court four years ago. I'm afraid they don't like me very much. Can't say I care much for them, either. Slimy bastards!"

Furst AGW Corporation was a multi-national conglomerate with tentacles reaching into all kinds of markets. But their primary business was in the energy sector. If there ever was a poster child for corporate greed and corruption, Furst AGW was it. Consumer advocate groups constantly picketed their offices. Furst AGW had been responsible for some of the worst environmental disasters of the twenty-first century.

"So now I've got this big, oily bull's eye painted on my back, and Furst AGW is gunning for me?"

"Let's not jump to conclusions, Carrie. If they wanted you dead, it figures that you'd be dead by now—like Winship. No, they want the technology, but they don't know enough about it yet."

Jake saw that Carrie was beginning to have problems hearing him over the crowd noise, so he moved closer to her. She cupped her hand around her ear. Jake cupped his hand around his mouth in turn.

"I'd guess that through their surveillance of Winship, Furst AGW knew Winship didn't have any significant breakthroughs yet. Perhaps they thought that their scientists could advance the science faster, or that Winship was becoming a nuisance. At any rate, they deemed him expendable. Now the bad news for Furst AGW is this: the legal assignment that Winship's law firm engineered is practically airtight, from what I can tell. AGW knows that they can't easily wrestle the property assignment away from you. They can certainly try bribing you as they tried with Winship. Ultimately, they can tie you up in court for years on appeals until they bleed you dry and you run out of money and can no longer fight. That won't get them what they want very quickly, though."

The good news for Furst AGW—and for that matter, for you too—I think, is that these materials have landed in the lap of one of the brightest minds in the country."

"What makes that good news?" asked Carrie, sounding brusque.

"Even though they didn't get anything new in ransacking your place, I'm sure they had better luck after tossing Winship's lab. They probably have everything that you started with. But I'm also guessing that their scientists are 'clueless in the zoo.' If I were they, I'd be betting on you to come through with the goods first."

Jake took a gulp.

"Carrie, *they* believe that you're the person who can unlock this puzzle for them and deliver on some sensational, new technology in the field of alternative energy."

Jake paused to down the remainder of his Margarita.

"That car missed you, right? I think they're just trying to scare you. You know what they say—'A miss is as good as a mile.'"

Carrie withdrew her cupped hand and frowned. Then she flipped Jake the bird in response.

Jake continued.

"That close encounter was the first shot across the bow. Our Mr. Gephardt's job offer-turned-fishing expedition was just underscoring the point that you're on their radar. Now, I'm certain they would assume you'd have them checked out. So it stands to reason that Premiere, a.k.a. Lockness, a.k.a. dot-dot-dot Furst AGW—wants you to know who they are, and that they're on to you."

"Oh! Okay, then!" replied Carrie, registering mock amazement. She was beginning to slur her words. "Now *I* know that… W-w-wait! I'll get this right: Now I know that '*They* know that *I* know that *they* know.' Did I get that right? Or maybe it's, '*I* know that *they* know that *I* know?' Hey! Either way, I feel a *whole lot better* knowing 'Who's on Furst.' Ha! Get it? 'Who's on Furst?'"

Carrie poked Jake in the chest with her finger for added emphasis, but the sudden move caused her to lose her balance. Carrie reached out her hand and put it on Jake's shoulder in an attempt to steady herself.

"Hey, sailor, wanna buy me another?"

Jake chuckled. "I don't think so, young lady. It's time for you to go home and go beddy-bye. My chariot awaits."

* * *

The following day, Jake arranged for an electronic eavesdropping inspection team to sweep Carrie's premises. There, the team found five devices expertly hidden in various rooms in Carrie's tiny apartment. There were two bugs in the bedroom alone.

"I don't know who these guys are, Jake, but they're good. They're using state-of-the-art hardware, newer stuff than most of the FBI offices are using. All of the serial numbers have been erased, of course, so that's a dead end."

Stewart Johnson summarized the results of his team's three-hour sweep to Jake over the phone.

"Thanks, Stewart. Go ahead, then, lock up and report your findings to Kenny if you would, please. He's tailing Carrie right now; he should be over at M.I.T. with her. You have his number, right?"

"Roger that," replied Stewart. "Say, should we…uh…Wait one!"

Jake could hear a raised voice in the background, followed by muffled discussion. A moment later, Stewart's voice returned on the line.

"Trouble! One of Bloomfield's neighbors just walked in on us. He has a key. He's demanding to know who we are. Won't tell us his name. What should we do? He's about to call the cops."

"Is his name Edward? Or Terrance?"

"Standby… Yeah. He says his name is Edward."

"Okay, put Edward on. Tell him, Carrie's 'karky fixer' wants to have a word with him." Jake chuckled in response to Stewart's next question.

"Never mind, *he'll* know what it means."

* * *

Carrie stopped to watch a girls' soccer match being played in Filipello Park in Watertown, just a few short blocks from the Alexandria Lighthouse Incubator. She liked to cut through the park on her way to and from The Lighthouse. Carrie had just wrapped up work on one of the few experiments unrelated to the Winship project.

It was a gorgeous Saturday morning; Carrie allowed herself this small luxury before heading off to her next stop. The fall foliage was spectacular in the small, urban park: the trees were turning brilliant shades of red, yellow and light tan. Most still had a sizeable portion of their leaves intact. Thirty to forty spectators—moms, dads, and smaller children – stood on the sidelines as they watched their teenage daughters and older sisters play on the field. Carrie watched them work the ball up and down the field, trading possession numerous times without a clear advantage or a shot from either team. From what she could see, it appeared that the two teams were pretty evenly matched.

She saw a small, black dog of mixed pedigree frolicking with a larger Chocolate Labrador Retriever. They stopped for a moment to sniff one another. Behind her, she saw an old man and woman sitting on a park bench speaking Armenian and sharing some sort of pastry. They must have been in their late 80s or early 90s. It was amazing how much they resembled one another. It looked to Carrie as though the couple had been together for a million years.

In Carrie's mind, everything—the people, Mother Nature, even the dogs—seemed to be in perfect balance at that moment.

Seeing the children at play made Carrie think of her brother,

William. He, Karen, and Dalisay seemed like the perfect family. They lived in a cute fixer-upper house in a quiet suburban neighborhood in Janesville. The family attended a Protestant church (was it Lutheran?) on a regular basis. That was Karen's influence, no doubt, since no one in Carrie's family—least of all William—had been even remotely religious.

William had two children from a previous marriage. But he and his current wife, Karen, seemed unable to conceive together. Karen was distraught. She blamed her husband, insisting that he was infertile. When they both underwent medical examinations, however, it turned out that Karen was the one who could not conceive, due to a malformation of her uterus. At one point, Karen had actually attempted suicide by taking an overdose of sleeping pills. Fortunately for the couple, Karen's pastor suggested that she and William consider adopting an orphan from overseas. They did just that; two years later, they were the proud parents of a beautiful four-year-old daughter from the Philippines.

Carrie recalled a heated discussion she had had a few years earlier with her sister-in-law about having children. Karen raised the question in front of Carrie whether women could experience a fulfilling life without bearing children. Moreover, she felt that it was a "mark of maturity and growth" for a woman to want to conceive and give birth. Karen hadn't actually accused Carrie of being immature, but it seemed to come damn close. Carrie responded by saying that she didn't feel the need to become a "breeder" in order to have a fulfilling life.

The conversation quickly degenerated from there. Karen opined what a shame it was that "someone as brilliant as you" would have no desire to pass on their genes to a new generation.

"Karen, if you *seriously* think I would risk passing on *these* genes," Carrie pointed to herself, "then you're nuts."

Karen frowned. She shook her head in an apparent show of pity, and replied, "Perhaps some day, Carrie, you will get past the pain and trauma of having your femininity taken from you…"

"Hey! Screw that crap!" Carrie was furious.

"Do you know what, Karen? You and I really aren't *all* that different: we both have big, ugly scars—except mine are on the *outside!*"

Carrie shook off those ugly thoughts from the encounter with her sister-in-law years ago, and returned to the present. She glanced over towards Arlington Street, where she spied a parked car she recognized: a late model blue Ford sedan. The occupant was a member of her security team.

Carrie thought it might be Dannie, but she wasn't positive. She should have felt reassured by his presence. But instead of feeling safer, the knowledge that this secret entourage shadowed her wherever she went, served as a constant reminder to her of just how vulnerable she really was.

She left the park, another very different vision of autumn displacing the earlier one, as she recollected the Mary Oliver poem that had struck her profoundly, and its compelling grim description of Blackwater Woods:

> *Every year*
> *Everything*
> *I have ever learned*
> *In my lifetime*
> *Leads back to this: the fires*
> *And the black river of loss . . .*

CHAPTER THIRTEEN

A not-so-subtle ringtone woke Carrie up from a sound sleep.

"DAH-duh-duh-DAH duh-duh dah…"

The melody was an audio clip from the movie, *Our Man Flint*, meant to alert the fictional secret agent of incoming calls on his 'red phone' from the President of the United States.

"Mmmm… What *is* that?" Paul asked groggily, wiping the sleep from his eyes. He rolled over carefully, unsure whether a cat was lying between them.

Carrie was already up, and throwing on her clothes from the previous evening.

"Sorry, sweetie. Work calls. One of my machines is in distress."

The machine to which Carrie referred was an Amnis ImageStream high-resolution cytometer located at the Whitehead Institute. Each of the instrument's two CCD cameras produced up to six images for a total of up to twelve images per cell. Each image could be used to calculate roughly 80 parameters to, among other things, show fluorescence strength and localization. Carrie was using it in her experiment to analyze a subset of cells from the Winship samples. She had programmed the high-end device to send out a text message if things got out of kilter. Carrie saw a diagnostic code showing that temperature levels in the machine's circuitry had risen above a safe threshold. Her first thought was that it could be indicative of a mechanical cooling failure—

probably a fan, or even a ventilation blockage. Whatever the case, the machine was a very valuable piece of equipment and she needed to get there quickly and resolve the problem.

Paul volunteered to give her a lift to the lab in his car.

"Go back to bed. You shouldn't have to lose sleep over this. It's my problem," she told him.

"Hey, it's no big deal. I'm happy to help. Besides, the sooner I get you in there to fix whatever it is, the sooner you can be back here and into this nice, warm bed with yours truly."

Paul rose from the bed to collect his clothes. As he walked by Carrie, he reached out and playfully swatted her on the behind.

* * *

At 4:30 a.m., it was easy for Paul to find a parking spot in the same block as the Institute. They parked and got out, and Paul keyed the alarm using his remote. Carrie waved at her "tail" that had parked down the street behind them, a half block away. She paused for a second to appreciate how quiet their surroundings were. No road noise, no honking cars, or delivery trucks—other than the one lone Boston Globe truck that sped by. It was in stark contrast to the hustle and bustle of the Kendall Square she was accustomed to. It was dark, too. The sun would not rise for another two hours. Carrie found herself thinking,

Perhaps I should start more of my mornings like this.

Carrie swiped the front door lock with her card. The two entered a stairwell and climbed to the second floor where the cytometer was situated.

"Here's the key, Paul—Room 213. Why don't you go on ahead and wait for me. Don't touch anything inside. I'll be right there. I need to pee."

* * *

Carrie washed her hands, and left the women's restroom. She took another moment to drink some water from the fountain, and then she strode down the hall toward the equipment room. When she was about five feet from the door, Carrie felt a rising panic. Suddenly, she realized its source.

CYANIDE!!!

Carrie was stopped in her tracks by the strong, sickly-sweet scent of cyanide gas.

She saw that the light to the room was turned on and the door was shut. She could only surmise that Paul had gone inside, unaware of the presence of the gas. The door would have closed automatically behind him.

Not everyone can easily smell cyanide. Her thesis advisor, Dr. O'Connor, had checked out all of his students in the beginning of their training to see if they could smell low levels of the deadly gas—a bottle of a cyanide solid chemical was opened. Mrs. Smiley then waved her hand over the inside of the bottle's screw cap, wafting air toward the testee. Mrs. Smiley winced, but Carrie smelled nothing. Carrie was then informed that, since she could not detect low levels of the odor, she was never to be alone in a lab when anyone was working in the chemical fume hood with the useful, but potentially lethal, substance. It was a basic safety rule. Terrified, she knew that for her to catch the suffocating odor at all, the concentration of cyanide gas had to be frighteningly high.

This was a dire emergency and there was no time for panic. Carrie knew that mere seconds could mean the difference between life and death. The emergency procedures drilled into her from graduate school automatically kicked in. Carrie quickly ran over to the nearest fire alarm and lifted up on the lever to activate it. The whooping noise was both reassuring and horrendous. Then she ran up the corridor looking for a first aid kit and any other safety items she could find. After racing about thirty feet, she saw the marked hallway closet containing safety and first aid equipment containing a half dozen oxygen masks and a basic first aid kit mounted on the wall. Unfortunately, the cyanide antidote kit was completely empty.

Dammit!!!

She grabbed one of the masks and quickly pulled it over her face and turned on the flow. With the first aid kit in one hand, and the second mask in the other, she bolted back down the hallway to room 213. She prayed it wasn't too late.

* * *

Carrie dragged Paul out of the room feet-first, and then she strapped the oxygen mask over his face. She turned the oxygen on full. Paul's skin had taken on a sickly, bright pinkish appearance. He appeared lifeless. She slapped his face hard a couple of times, but saw no response from him. She did detect a weak pulse, however. As she took Paul's and her masks off momentarily and applied mouth-to-mouth resuscitation, the suffocating sweet scent filled her nose. Then she reseated both masks.

Seconds later, out of the corner of her eye she saw a short, stocky Indian man. She recognized him; he worked as a postdoc in a lab down the hall. The man came around the corner, walking quickly in her direction. When he spotted her, he froze. He looked frightened.

Carrie stood up, and waved him back with both arms, shouting, "Gas! Gas! Gas!" as loudly as she could. She wasn't sure if he could hear her over the whelping of the alarm. Also, the oxygen mask muffled her voice. But he must have surmised fairly quickly what was going on. He backed away from her, turned around, and ran as though he'd seen a ghost.

* * *

"No, I didn't get a call from a person, the *machine* sent me a text message!"

Carrie was starting to get exasperated with the inane questions asked of her by Detective Sergeant John Hatherley of the Cambridge Police Department. It seemed to her as though Hatherley was purposely being dense.

This guy has watched too many episodes of Columbo, she fumed.

The detective appeared to be wearing the same clothes from the day before. His shirt had a slight coffee stain and his collar was bent back. It had an awkward crease where one shouldn't have been.

"Okay, Doctor, so the *machine* sent you this message because it had *exceeded its…operating…parameters.*" The cop emphasized the last few words carefully, as though he was not used to saying multisyllabic words. "I see. Now—how did it *know* where to route the message?"

"It's very simple, Detective Hatherley. As I said earlier, I programmed the instrument to do it. It's very smart, you see? It costs a quarter of a million bucks. It's *almost* as smart as some people I've met."

There was an unmistakable air of sarcasm in her voice.

"But if you want to know every last minutia of detail, it's because I selected menu item number two, followed by menu item number five, and then I punched in my cell phone number, 6-1-7, 3-1-2…JESUS!"

Carrie blew up at him. "Do I really have to explain this? Listen— why don't you ask me something that's actually pertinent, like, 'Do you know where the cyanide gas came from?!'"

Carrie looked beyond the detective, at the multitude of law enforcement people assembled in the building lobby. Several of them stopped their conversations momentarily and glanced at the pair to see what the commotion was about. She spotted members of the M.I.T. Police Department, Cambridge Police, Cambridge Fire, the Massachusetts State Police, and a full HazMat team along with a few other plainclothes types whose affiliations were unclear. They all looked as though they either wanted another cup of coffee, or there was someplace else they'd rather be. She shouted at the assembled throng:

"Hey!! Can anybody tell me how Paul Santiago is doing? You know—the 'vic?'"

One of the plain-clothes officers nodded at her, and then he pulled out his cell phone and called the hospital.

Moments later, a new face arrived on the scene. A short, middle-aged, bald African-American man wearing a badge was working his way through the assembled mass of law enforcement. He approached Carrie and the Detective Sergeant. In contrast to *Columbo*, the man was impeccably dressed in an expensive-looking dark suit. He sported a crisp, red bow tie.

After a few seconds, Carrie recognized him.

"Detective Sergeant, Dr. Bloomfield," he nodded. "I'm Robert Foster, Special Agent In Charge of the FBI Boston office."

"Pleased to meet you, Mister Special Agent In Charge. My name's John Hatherley, Detective Sergeant, at your service. So, what brings you out on this fine morning to the Mecca of Geekdom?"

Foster ignored the detective; he turned to Carrie.

"Dr. Bloomfield, it's a pleasure to see you again. I only wish it was under more pleasant circumstances. First of all—are you okay?"

Before she could answer, the man with the cell phone approached. He addressed Carrie.

"Uhh, Dr. Bloomfield, sorry to interrupt. That was the emergency room desk at Mass General. Your friend, Paul Santiago...he's...I'm sorry. He didn't make it."

Carrie was dumbstruck. Seconds passed. To Carrie, time seemed to stand still. Foster finally spoke.

"Hatherley, give us a minute. Okay?"

"Sure, whatever," he muttered, strolling away without so much as an "I'm sorry."

"Is there some place we could go and sit down for a few minutes?" asked Foster.

"No...uhh...Yes, there's a...there's a break room down the hall," she said. Was it just yesterday that she had remembered the Mary Oliver poem, the one that spoke of fires, and a black river of loss, when she had felt the sudden upheaval of a bright autumn day through which a dark spectre was rising?

* * *

Special Agent in Charge Robert Foster was only too happy to become involved in the investigation. Not only did it fall clearly within the Bureau's jurisdiction, Jake Shapiro was a good friend of Foster's, and a former classmate from Harvard Law School. They played squash together on a regular basis. Plus, Carrie Bloomfield was a gutsy woman;

she had once performed a huge service for Foster, and other agents from the Bureau of Alcohol, Tobacco, Firearms and Explosives. As far as Foster was concerned, he owed her one.

When Jake received the early morning phone call from Carrie's security tail—and then Carrie—about the crisis, Jake had called Robert Foster immediately to ask for the Bureau's involvement. As Robert drove from his Milton home to the M.I.T. campus, Jake filled him in over the phone about the mysterious death of the prominent Woods Hole scientist, the materials he had arranged to send to Carrie, and also, his suspicions about Furst AGW.

Foster and Carrie reached the break room. He fed some dollar bills into the vending machine and selected two Diet Cokes. He handed one to Carrie, and then he sat down in the chair next to her. Foster said nothing; instead, he patiently waited for Carrie to speak when she was ready.

"I'm responsible, Robert. If *only* I had *just* gone to the bathroom at home first instead of here, or told him to wait outside I would have been with him and I could have warned him."

"That doesn't make it your fault, Carrie. It was simply bad luck."

Foster listened some more. After a few minutes, Carrie seemed more composed and focused. Foster felt that it was okay to ask her some questions.

"Can you tell me the potential uses for potassium cyanide in a laboratory setting?"

"Well, it's not used that widely—at least, not anymore. I'd say, only three or four labs in the whole building use the stuff. One lab uses cyanide in their studies of cellular respiration. Sometimes it's used in manufacturing, but no one does that here."

"I'm told that about 80 percent of males have the ability to detect cyanide with their olfactory glands. That percentage is even higher for women, correct?"

"That's right. It's estimated that 90 to 95 percent of all females can smell cyanide," Carrie added, "But I can't smell low levels. Bad genetics." She hugged herself tightly across her breastless chest.

"So, Carrie… How many people in this building do you suppose might know whether you personally *can* smell cyanide gas?"

Her eyes widened as the implications of the question sank in.

"Most of the P.I.s in the building probably have the memo from the safety office containing the names of the lab people who can detect a cyanide odor. But it's not an 'all-or-nothing' thing. It varies by degree."

"The State Police's HazMat crew said there was an unusually large quantity of potassium cyanide in the room—far more than one would normally have on hand for research purposes. Is it stockpiled somewhere in the building?"

"No, I don't think so," replied Carrie. "I believe it's purchased in small quantities on an as-needed basis, and stored in secure locations within each lab that uses it. As I said, only a few use the stuff. And of those that do, they use only minute amounts. Given the quantity the HazMat guys are describing, I have no idea where it came from."

"And so it's safe to say that no one would ever leave potassium cyanide crystals lying around unattended on purpose?"

"They're kept in the labs with the other chemicals. But they're labeled so you know the danger."

"Who would dump them into a large container of acid and leave the container unattended?"

"No one! And no one would work with cyanide alone." She shook her head, hugged herself tighter. No one handles cyanide there. There's no chemical fume hood."

Foster thought for a moment.

"You know, Jake has a working theory about all of this. He believes it's connected to that outfit, Furst AGW. He thinks that they're trying to intimidate you. Jake told me about the break-in and the incident with the van; also, the call with the phony job offer. My office is taking lead in this case. It's now officially 'an act of domestic terrorism.' By the way, I'll see what I can do about keeping 'Andy of Mayberry' from hassling you further."

Carrie raised her eyes briefly to Foster's.

Foster added, "Jake will be here shortly. He'll see to it that you get home. I believe that he also intends to add an additional security team to your watch. Carrie, I'm really sorry about Paul. Jake told me that you two were close."

Carrie's eyes welled up with tears. She tried as best as she could to retain her composure, but the stress and the horror of the morning's events were finally catching up with her. She felt vulnerable and also, completely spent. Carrie knew that she would not be able to keep her emotions in check, so she stood up, preparing to flee the room. Robert stood up, in turn. He reached over to her, his arms outstretched, to offer her solace in a hug. Carrie accepted.

Seconds later, she broke into sobs. The tears fell from her like a torrential river. There were the broken words of the poem again, describing the black river of loss "…whose other side is salvation, whose meaning we will never know… Bereft and shattered within a landscape where no pieces fit," she sobbed anew.

* * *

Robert Foster was just nine years old when he first decided to be a lawman. Of course, many young boys dream of becoming a policeman or a fireman, but Robert had a role model whom he could emulate: his father, Randall Foster, was a Deputy Sheriff in Shelby County, Tennessee in the 50s and 60s. Randall Foster's position was highly unusual. The elder Foster was, perhaps, one of only a handful of colored law enforcement officers in the entire south at that time.

Robert was raised in a large, loving family with six siblings. He loved the usual sorts of outdoor activities that young boys enjoy. But he was also a very cerebral young man: he excelled in all manner of puzzles and brainteasers; and he absolutely loved chess. Robert even taught his sixth grade teacher how to play the game. He excelled academically throughout middle school.

When he was a freshman in high school, his principal encouraged Robert to apply for a scholarship to Phillips Academy, a prestigious boarding school in Andover, Massachusetts. Robert was accepted; he left his home in Tennessee to live and study in the affluent Boston suburb.

Like most of the students at Phillips Academy, Robert was groomed to attend the hallowed halls of an Ivy League institution. He chose Harvard University where he majored in pre-law, graduating *cum laude* in just three years. He was readily accepted into Harvard Law School in the same graduating class as Jake Shapiro. The two were roommates in the HLS graduate housing, and despite their age difference, they also became best friends. Unlike Jake, who went on to become a patent litigation attorney, Robert never completely outgrew his childhood fantasy of becoming a lawman. Only two years out of Harvard, he left the small firm where he was a junior associate, and applied to become an agent with the Federal Bureau of Investigation.

* * *

Special Agent in Charge Robert Foster wasted no time opening a full-scale investigation into the attack at the Whitehead Institute that had killed Paul Santiago.

Authorities shut down the building for twenty-four hours while evidence was gathered, and HazMat crews finished their cleanup. Foster's team began interviewing the various principle investigators, along with their lab personnel.

"Carrie, we compiled a list of six people who accessed the door with their keycards between 5:00 p.m. of the previous evening and 5:00 a.m. on the morning of the attack. Now, this person, here—" Robert pulled out a glossy black and white photo and showed it to Carrie. "Chulbul Roy. Do you recognize him?"

"Yes, that's him. Chulbul. He's the man I saw while I was trying to save Paul. He's a postdoc; he works in Dr. Sorinson's lab, I think."

"He swiped in at around midnight. You're *sure* he's the individual you saw at around 4:55 a.m. that morning in the hallway?"

"Yes. I'm positive. I shouted at him that there was gas, and waved him away. He looked at me for a moment, and then he turned around and ran. Odd…"

"What's that, Carrie?"

"The alarm had been sounding for several minutes at that point. And there are two other emergency exits much closer to his lab door; both are in the opposite direction."

"That's good information, Carrie. We'll be sure to ask him that question. As I said, there are six names on this list, including yours. Over the next day or two, Roy and the others will be given polygraph tests. I hope you won't take offense at this—but, would you be willing to submit to a polygraph test, also?"

Carried didn't hesitate. "Of course, Robert. I know I need to be tested too."

* * *

"Dr. Bloomfield, please come in. My name is Art Stephens. I'm a civilian employed by the Bureau's Boston office. Before you sit down, please hold this wiring harness for me—like so—thank you. Now, excuse me, please."

Stephens walked behind Carrie, and then he reached around in front of her, taking the harness from her hands. Stephens then wrapped the harness around the front of her upper abdomen. He fastened two straps together against her lower back. They made a loud snapping noise.

Stephens continued with his wiring. He attached electrodes to her arms and forehead. When he was finished, he motioned to Carrie to sit down. He went back to his station, and sat in front of his console to make some final adjustments to the equipment. As he was doing so, he asked Carrie:

"Tell me, Doctor, have you ever taken a polygraph test before?"

"No—well, actually—yes. I have."

Carrie described to Stephens a psychology experiment she had participated in once as an undergraduate at the University of Wisconsin. For the tidy sum of twenty dollars, she signed up as an experimental subject. As with most psychology experiments, the test subject was not told the true nature of the experiment until after its completion. And sometimes, the experiment's purpose was not revealed even then; for fear that the subjects would tell other would-be test subjects about the experiment, thus skewing the results.

Carrie could not figure out at the time what the graduate student conducting the experiment was trying to accomplish. He told Carrie that his work involved developing new algorithms to improve a polygraph's accuracy. Perhaps he was being completely honest with her.

Carrie recalled trying her utmost to fool the device. She even went so far as to 'self-hypnotize' herself into believing that her birthday was September 23, instead of March 23; and that she had been born in Milwaukee, Wisconsin instead of Los Angeles. She reckoned that those questions—which she answered truthfully on the intake questionnaire—would establish a "baseline" and thus, would be considered mandatory during the questioning.

Carrie was correct in her assumption. The examiner—a second-year graduate student working on his doctorate in psychology—asked if her birthday was on March 23. When she replied in the affirmative, her mind was racing with the implanted thought that it was really in September and that she had just fibbed to him! The examiner looked at his readout, and then he paused. He seemed genuinely puzzled. Carrie rewarded herself with a quick little smile. She knew that she had fooled the machine. But a few questions later, he asked Carrie about her place of birth. She replied, "yes" to Los Angeles, California while thinking, "Milwaukee." Unfortunately, though, the questioner didn't pause or miss a beat. This time he went right on to the next question. Carrie figured she was unsuccessful at pulling off the ruse that second time.

* * *

"Is your name Jane Bloomfield?"

"No."

"Is your name Carrie Bloomfield?"

"Yes."

"Do you hold a Doctor of Philosophy degree in Biological Chemistry from Harvard University?"

"Yes."

"Do you hold a Bachelor of Science degree from UCLA?"

"No."

"Do you hold a Doctor of Philosophy degree in Biological Chemistry from the Massachusetts Institute of Technology?"

"No."

"Are you employed by the Massachusetts Institute of Technology?"

Carrie paused for a brief moment, and then she replied, "Technically, no. I hold several Visiting Staff Scientist appointments at M.I.T. labs and affiliates, but they're 'courtesy appointments' only. I'm not a paid employee."

Stephens checked off a box on his clipboard.

"I see. We'll skip that question for now."

"Have you handled potassium cyanide within the past four weeks?"

"Yes."

Stevens looked up at Carrie, eyeing her suspiciously, waiting for an explanation.

"I don't normally work with potassium cyanide in any of my experiments. But two weeks ago, I found a small bottle of potassium cyanide that someone had left sitting in the common equipment area. It was labeled as Dr. Cosner's. His lab *does* work with it. I put the bottle back where it belonged."

Stephens was apparently satisfied with the explanation.

"Did you prepare—or were you involved in the preparation of a potassium cyanide-acid mixture in Room 258 of the Whitehead Institute, that led to the death of…"

"No!! I didn't," she interrupted. "No. Sorry."

"That's alright, Doctor. I'm going to ask you to try to keep calm. I'll repeat the question again in a moment. Please wait until I've finished stating a question in its entirety *before* you answer 'yes' or 'no.' Okay?"

Carrie nodded.

"Is your middle name 'Elizabeth'?"

"Yes."

"Do you currently own a motor vehicle?"

"No."

"Did you prepare—or were you involved in the preparation of— a potassium cyanide-acid mixture in Room 258 of the Whitehead Institute that led to the death of Paul Santiago?"

Carrie answered calmly this time.

"No."

"Have you ever been convicted of a crime?"

"No."

"Were you born in Milwaukee, Wiscon…?"

Stephens stopped himself. He recalled Carrie's story about her encounter with the polygraph in college, and her ruse with Milwaukee. Stephens and Carrie both chuckled over the choice of the distracter question-and-answer that he had prepared earlier quite by coincidence.

"We'll skip that question."

Stephens turned off the machine, and then he stood up, motioning her to do likewise.

"I'm done now, Carrie," he said, as he began taking the wiring harness off her body. "It should come as no surprise that you passed with flying colors."

"It's a good thing you stopped when you did," quipped Carrie. "You know, I probably would have *had* you there on Milwaukee."

The next individual Stephens questioned that afternoon wasn't so careful about telling the truth.

* * *

A week after the attack at the Whitehead Institute, Edward and Terrance Smith-Hughes accompanied Carrie to New Jersey for Paul Santiago's wake and funeral. Insofar as Edward and Terrance were concerned, there were no ifs, ands or buts—Carrie had been there for the couple in their time of joyous celebration, therefore they would not let her suffer through this tragedy alone. Carrie paid for the car rental, but she allowed the two to drive her.

Carrie was quiet—lost in her thoughts for most of the drive. Edward had tried to cheer her up for a good portion of the trip, but he finally gave up somewhere along the Taconic State Parkway. It didn't take the therapist in Terrance to see that Carrie was grieving. He kept his mouth shut, but he reached over and gave Carrie's arm a squeeze. She smiled, weakly.

126

Paul Santiago was the middle child in a family of five siblings who grew up in Bayonne, New Jersey. Paul's father had died five years earlier; his mother, Anna Marie, was fifty-nine years old—only six years older than Carrie. Paul was also survived by a grandmother, three sisters, two brothers, and five nieces and nephews.

Over a hundred family and friends attended the wake. Many of Paul's family came over to Carrie and gave her a hug. Although Paul had not spoken very much about Carrie to his immediate family, some knew that the young artist had fallen in love with a woman from Boston who worked as a scientist. What they hadn't known, however, was that Paul was significantly younger than she. If any of his family members blamed Carrie for Paul's death, they did not say or do anything to indicate that was the case. The Santiagos were a loving family. They shared their grief openly, as they did their affection for one another.

The family had asked Carrie to bring with her some of Paul's paintings to display at the wake. They were proud of their Paulie, the artist. Carrie had asked Edward if he would visit Paul's small studio apartment in Somerville and select a few of Paul's paintings to bring along. Besides, Carrie rationalized, Edward was a fellow artist; he would know which paintings were more significant and therefore, would best honor Paul's memory. In reality, she could not bear to bring herself to visit his flat. The wounds were too fresh.

When she walked into the side parlor in the funeral home in which Paul's paintings had been set up, Carrie glanced at the artwork, and then she stopped in her tracks. Among the six pieces, Edward had selected one she had never seen before. It stood out prominently. It was an unfinished charcoal sketch of a nude, female figure. The figure's chest was adorned with that familiar, stylish genie coming out of a bottle. Unlike her own likeness, however, Carrie saw that the figure had been given breasts. The figure beckoned the viewer with its eyes, and by the sensuous shape of its mouth, as if it was saying,

Come! I have a secret to share!

Just then, Paul's mother Ann Marie walked up alongside Carrie. She, too, was drawn strongly to the sketch. She remarked, "What an interesting sketch. Wasn't he talented?"

"Yes, ma'am, he certainly was."

"Please, Carrie, call me Ann Marie. I'm sorry that we're meeting one another for the first time under such tragic circumstances."

Carrie turned to face Ann Marie. The woman was short and petite, olive skinned, with a head full of long, thick, dark hair. She wore a modest, black dress. Carrie thought she looked quite young for her age.

Carrie tried to force a smile.

A moment passed; the two women walked silently as they viewed the remaining pieces of art, but both shared a deep connection to the charcoal sketch. Eventually they both gravitated back to it, as though beckoned.

Finally, Ann Marie spoke again. She said, softly,

"That's *you* in the sketch, isn't it, dear?"

Carrie started to sob quietly.

"He must have loved you very much. It shows in how he drew you so lovingly."

The moment was excruciating for Carrie.

"I...I..."

How do I tell a mother that her son would be alive today were it not for the fact that I sent him to his death?

Carrie blurted out, "I'm so sorry!" Then she hurried away quickly in search of the ladies' room.

CHAPTER FOURTEEN

Carrie Bloomfield had not always been an academic gadfly. Shortly after her last postdoctoral position she had made the jump into industry to work for Vital Biosphere, Inc., a privately held firm situated along the Route 128 corridor in Waltham, Massachusetts. VBI produced diagnostic products to detect toxins in the industrial market. During her tenure there, Carrie rose quickly through the ranks. She started as a Senior Research Scientist. Later she was promoted to Director of Research. Not long after, she was named Vice President and Chief Scientific Officer for VBI. Carrie was responsible for all of R&D and Technical Services. She reported to the Chief Executive Officer and Founder, Jack Beasley. She was employed by VBI for almost ten years.

The work was both exciting and challenging. It was financially rewarding as well. During VBI's heyday in the 90s, Carrie was responsible for over 100 employees on the organizational chart, along with six direct reports. VBI controlled a 40 percent market share worldwide and a 60 percent domestic market in the toxin detection industry.

Carrie was reasonably satisfied with her career at VBI. Sure, there were the usual headaches and screw-ups that come with the job, like a domineering and sometimes stubborn boss; or, bench scientists and technicians who—while competent in their little worlds—would frequently behave irrationally and exhibit anti-social behavior. There was also the near-catastrophic contamination of their entire product inventory due to the incompetence of her QA Manager. To top it off, there was the one time when she had to deal with a scientist who was prone to saying very inappropriate things to women. Carrie was able to cleverly finesse him into tendering his resignation, before charges of sexual harassment were filed against the company.

All in all, though, life was good for Carrie Bloomfield at VBI until the day that the corporate culture abruptly changed for the worse. Carrie recalled that it felt a bit like when someone bumps a phonograph player, sending the arm and its needle flying across the record's surface while playing one's favorite song. In the summer of 1998, nepotism reared its ugly head in the form of one Suzanna Beasley, who came to work for VBI. She was the CEO's daughter.

Suzanna Beasley—a.k.a. "Suzie"—arrived from Silicon Valley amid lots of fanfare and celebration. She liked to smile a lot, and show off her bleached white teeth. Suzie could also set the world record in the head-nodding department. She had read somewhere in a book on managing people that an affirmative nod was the single most important gesture one could make, because it communicated to the other person that one was fully engaged with him or her. As a result, a face-to-face conversation with Suzie could result in the other person's feeling seasick if they focused too closely on her head movements.

Suzie possessed a lavish wardrobe of flashy designer clothes. She would show up each day at work wearing brightly colored attire from the high-end brands like Dolce & Gabbana, or the French label, Cacharel. The other women joked that Suzie's closet didn't contain a single skirted suit.

Plus, her hair was perfect.

Suzie had attended Brandeis University, earning a Bachelor's degree in Marketing. After graduation, she headed for the west coast to find her fame and fortune. Suzie worked for several computer companies as a marketing dweeb. Along the way, she picked up her 'trophy husband'—Janssen—a muscular body builder of Dutch descent who had emigrated from South Africa. He was employed from time to time as a personal trainer to the stars. She and Janssen had two children, Sally and

Curtis. Suzie made sure they never wanted for anything. Consequently, Sally and Curtis were both thoroughly spoiled.

Suzie had climbed the corporate ladder to become a mid-level marketing manager at Xitex, a firm that specialized in producing and selling business software. Initially, everyone at Xitex thought that Suzie would be a rising star. Indeed, Suzie had the knack for "walking the walk" and "talking the talk." But, ultimately, those skills got her only so far. Suzie explained to her friends and family that she had hit the proverbial glass ceiling that so many women in business faced at some point in their careers. Xitex's corporate officers didn't view it that way, however. As far as they were concerned, Suzie had hit a ceiling all right—the "competency ceiling." Suzie's promotions suddenly stopped, and her annual pay raises shrank with each passing year. Suzie saw the handwriting on the wall.

Fortunately for her, though, Daddy was the founder and CEO of a successful biotechnology company in Boston. Upon hearing of his daughter's plight, the elder Beasley welcomed Suzie and her family back home to Beantown with open arms (especially his two precious grandchildren, but to a much lesser extent, his son-in-law). Human Resources at VBI were instructed to arrange for Suzie to be hired into the newly created position of Senior Vice President of Marketing. Suzie put their Santa Cruz home on the market, and she instructed her unemployed hubby to stay in California to manage the sale—for however long it might take. Meanwhile, with Daddy's help, Suzie purchased a very nice colonial with six bedrooms and three and half baths in the upscale Boston suburb of Lincoln. She exclaimed to mum and dad, "The kids and I simply adore it!"

* * *

"I think you now have a person of interest."

Art Stephens laid the memo down on the desk of the Special Agent in Charge of the Boston FBI Field Office, Robert Foster.

Foster picked up the memo and stared at it for a moment. Then he glanced up at Stephens.

"Chulbul Roy, huh?"

"Yes. He's the postdoc who came face to face with Carrie in the hallway during the attack. Of course, we had several nervous Nellies among the bunch who were borderline on certain questions. But the results from Dr. Roy's exam are unquestionable. I got strong readings on the distracters, and even stronger stress readings on the questions about the cyanide. He failed rather impressively."

"Excellent work, Art. Thanks. I'll have our guys pick up the good doctor for further questioning."

* * *

Chulbul Roy sat anxiously in the small FBI interrogation room at One Plaza on Cambridge Street in downtown Boston. The room was barely large enough to accommodate a small table and two uncomfortable-looking folding chairs. Looking at Roy through the one-way glass, Foster could see that he was visibly nervous and ill at ease. Foster would let Agent Sandra Mallory take a go at him first. He would follow up with a second round of questioning, if necessary.

Mallory had been with the Boston team for just six months, and she was still learning the ropes. Although Mallory had been a witness to several interrogations, this one would be her first time interrogating a suspect. Foster thought it was time for her to get her feet wet with a major case.

* * *

"Dr. Roy, thank you for taking the time to come in so that we can clear up a few loose ends," said Mallory, as she entered the room with a pen and a pad of paper. She seated herself.

"Certainly. I will do my best to describe what I saw," replied the portly Indian man. His English was thickly accented with Assamese, one of the more common languages spoken in his native country.

"So, according to the statement you gave to the police that morning, you had not gone near the machine room where the potassium cyanide spill occurred until after the alarm sounded. Is that correct?"

"Yes, that is correct. I heard the fire alarm. Before exiting the building, I thought to go down the hall to check on others. I saw a man walking down the hallway in that direction only five minutes or so before the alarm sounded."

"I see," replied Mallory. She paused for a moment, and rubbed her temples as though she was attempting to dispel a troubling thought.

"Dr. Roy, how many pairs of shoes do you own?"

Roy chuckled, and then he replied, "Not many. I can't afford much of a wardrobe on my salary. Three, I think—my running sneakers, a pair of wingtip dress shoes, and these."

Roy pointed under the table, to a pair of casual shoes he was wearing.

"Were you wearing these shoes on the morning of the attack?"

Roy's face took on a puzzled look.

"Yes, I think so. Why?"

"Those are Dexter shoes, right? It's their 'Skecher Work' model. About a nine-and-a-half? Plus, you have a little gouge on the lower right-hand side of the heel of your left shoe? Do you want to know how I know this, Doctor?"

She paused for a split second and, not waiting for an answer, Agent Mallory continued with her monologue.

"We know that the floor was mopped clean by the janitor around 8:30 p.m. the evening before. Interestingly, however, we found a thin film of residue coating the floor near the bottle of acid. They tell me it was sodium bicarbonate. The film contained a partial shoe print.

"Did you know that sodium bicarbonate is used to neutralize acid? Acid, like the kind that someone accidentally spilled on the floor prior to mixing it with potassium cyanide crystals to produce the gas. But, of course, you would know all of this, wouldn't you? You're a scientist. Oh, and the bicarbonate? We found the discarded shipping container that it came in. It was in the dumpster out back. Interesting—the container was shipped to you. It had your name on it."

"This may come as a surprise to you, Dr. Roy, but we think *you're* the person responsible for the attack. Yesterday, you utterly failed your polygraph test. That fact alone is enough for us to obtain a search warrant and to go up your ass with a proctoscope."

Mallory leaned forward over the table and pressed her face close to his as she voiced her threat.

"We will toss your world upside down, Roy. Do you understand me? We will build an ironclad case against you. You will be charged with domestic terrorism and capital murder. You will be tried and found guilty in a court of law and you *will* spend the rest of your life behind bars. With your numerous girlfriends."

Mallory backed away from Roy, and sat back in her chair. There was slight hint of a smirk on her face.

"Oh, by the way, I want to thank you for saving us the time and trouble by bringing those shoes in with you today. Now we won't have to go over to your apartment to retrieve them."

Roy looked dumbfounded. He glanced down at the table, and then he shut his eyes tightly, as though he was attempting to wish away a bad dream.

Foster continued to listen in, and observe them through the glass. Mallory had done very well. It appeared to Foster as though Roy was on the verge of tears.

A long minute passed.

Roy glanced up from the table at Mallory. Then, he glanced over to the mirror on the wall, behind which Foster stood, as though he was searching for something.

Foster thought, *Uh-oh. This is where he's going to lawyer up.*

Roy took a deep breath, and then he turned back to face Agent Mallory.

"I want to make a deal. I have information."

* * *

It was a bright, sunny day on the morning of September 28, 1999. Carrie Bloomfield, Vice President of R&D at VBI, pulled her aging Saab into the company parking lot. Immediately, she saw that something was terribly amiss: fire apparatus from the Waltham Fire

Department's Tower Ladder One and Engine Two were on scene. Their red strobe lights cast a pulsating reflection against the windows and front door. Rescue Six was just arriving on scene at the west gate of the parking lot, as Carrie exited her vehicle. Carrie noticed a small crowd of a dozen VBI employees milling around at a distance in the parking lot. One of the lab technicians, Jane Laughton, spotted Carrie, and walked over to her.

"What's up, Jane?"

"I'm not sure, Carrie. They think it might be a gas leak. The firemen aren't telling us anything. They say they're waiting for a company manager to …"

Just then, Carrie's pager beeped. She saw that the number belonged to Suzie Beasley, the boss's daughter.

She's probably calling to get an update. I'll deal with her later, Carrie thought.

A fireman walked up to where Carrie and Jane Loughton were standing. He addressed Carrie.

"Excuse me. Miss? They told me you're in charge here."

The question—actually, more of a statement—came from Waltham Fire Lieutenant Max Burwell.

"Well, I guess I'm the senior ranking manager on the premises at the moment. My name is Carrie Bloomfield. I head up Research and Development here."

"I'm Lieutenant Burwell. Can we speak somewhere privately, Ms. Bloomfield? We have a…situation here."

Jane spoke up. "I'll leave you two to speak privately." She nodded to both of them. "*Doctor*. Lieutenant."

* * *

Lieutenant Burwell explained to Carrie what the firefighters were confronted with. At 7:15 A.M., a lab technician had arrived at work and entered the lab. He detected the strong odor of gas. Upon further examination, he found several gas jets had been left turned on. The technician quickly shut off the flow. After doing so, he noticed several long, thin wires running from the door handles of a lab door. They were attached to three devices of unknown origin sitting on the counter top. The technician immediately set off the fire alarm and exited the lab through a different door. When firefighters arrived on the scene, the man warned them about entering, having described to them what he had seen.

"See that guy? Right over there, Doctor. Yeah. Wearing the blue shirt and grey pants. Says his name is Kyle Simpson."

Carrie knew Kyle on sight. In fact, she knew him only too well. She and Kyle had had a rather unpleasant meeting the day before.

* * *

Kyle Simpson was a bright young man. He had earned his Bachelor's degree in Chemistry, but for reasons known only to him, Kyle had stopped short of applying to graduate school, thus seriously limiting his career options in the sciences.

Kyle had dropped by Carrie's office unannounced to tell Carrie that he was angry and upset. He was considering accepting a job offer with a biotech firm in Cambridge. Kyle told her that the job paid almost $20,000 more annually than what VBI was currently paying him. Kyle had "respectfully requested" a raise of a comparable amount. In exchange for the raise, Kyle told Carrie that he would decline the new job offered to him by the Cambridge firm and he would continue his contract with VBI. Further, Kyle hinted that he would not pursue any future discrimination charges against Carrie or VBI.

Carrie took only about ten seconds to formulate her reply.

"Kyle, I think the new position sounds like a wonderful opportunity for you. It obviously would be in your best interests to accept their offer. So, good luck."

Kyle seemed stunned. After a second, he replied, "Would you be willing to write a positive letter of recommendation on my behalf, Carrie?"

"Why would you need *that*, Kyle? I thought you said they've already made you the offer?"

* * *

Carrie was pretty certain why Kyle had attempted the ploy. Through the lab gossip, Carrie learned Kyle had met privately with Suzie to express his unhappiness over the poor job performance review he had received a month earlier. Kyle felt that he didn't deserve the black mark, and that he was being treated unfairly because he was a man. Besides, Kyle informed her, he was a "better performer than most of the other lab techs"—meaning the women.

Suzie thrived on this sort of conflict. Although VBI had a Human Resources department, Suzie jumped at the opportunity to mediate this perceived crisis. With her head bobbing up and down at a whooping crane's pace, Suzie told Kyle that she understood his plight. She agreed wholeheartedly with Kyle. She set out to soothe Kyle's fragile ego, and to assure him that she would personally investigate the incident involving the poor review he had received from Carrie Bloomfield.

* * *

"So Kyle Simpson discovered this, Lieutenant?

"Yes, Doctor."

"Please, call me Carrie. I'm not big into titles."

"Okay, Carrie. Me neither. Call me Max. So, how well do you know this Kyle guy? 'Cuz I'm getting a funny feelin' about him. I don't think he's being straight with us."

Max explained to Carrie that in his years on the job, he'd seen this sort of thing before: guys who light the match, and then call the fire department so that they could be seen as the hero.

"He may be a great guy and a hard worker, Carrie, but he's raising all kinds of red flags in my gut."

"You're wise to be suspicious of him, Max. I'll tell you why."

* * *

Carrie received an earful from Suzie about the poor performance review, just days before Kyle met with Carrie about his intentions to walk. Suzie reminded Carrie that there was such a thing as "reverse discrimination" and the management at VBI "needs to be careful about this sort of thing."

"Now, I'm not saying you consciously did anything wrong, Carrie. Maybe Kyle did mess up a time or two. And perhaps his attitude towards his peers could be better. But can you honestly say that you and your direct report have judged Kyle in the same way that you judge the other lab technicians—especially the female techs?"

"Actually, yes, Suzie. I *can* say that. He was judged fairly and impartially."

Carrie added, "Need I remind you that Kyle's immediate supervisor is male *and* that Kyle has a previous reprimand in his file from last year involving an incident witnessed by at least four other people—two male, two female."

Suzie responded immediately. "Well, I still think you should give Kyle another chance. It'd be a terrible thing if we were to lose him. Bad. You know, bad for lab morale. And with all the belt-tightening that's going on around here, well, if Kyle is unhappy enough to actually leave VBI, I'm not sure that we can guarantee you an open requisition with which to hire his replacement…"

Suzie left that last statement dangling in the air. As if to underscore its importance, her head had ceased its incessant nodding, and her eyes narrowed on her last few words. For Carrie, it was unmistakably a threat.

"Suzie, tell me, what *exactly* is your interest in this matter? If Kyle feels he's been wronged, shouldn't you be referring him to Sarah Broadman in HR?"

Suzie's frozen smile broke, transforming itself into a dour frown. Without saying another word, she stood up and shot out of Carrie's office.

Screw you! Carrie thought.

* * *

As more employees began to arrive that morning, so, too, did law enforcement. Within the hour, there were over sixty officers and firefighters on the scene. Several additional agencies had sent personnel: Waltham Police and the Massachusetts State Police's bomb disposal unit, along with the agents from ATF and the FBI. Jack Beasley pulled in shortly after the federal agents arrived. Beasley's daughter, Suzie, eventually arrived at around 9:15 a.m. Television crews from channels four, five, and seven were also on-scene. Their trucks were parked a block away. Each of the truck's hydraulic-powered microwave towers was fully erected, standing by to beam "action news" back to their studios. Camera crews were making last minute sound checks, and small adjustments to their lighting; they were almost ready to go "live" with reports to hungry television audiences.

By 9:35 a.m. agency leaders were huddled up in the far corner of the parking lot along with the senior VBI management consisting of Jack, Suzie and Carrie. Lieutenant Burwell was the designated on-scene incident commander.

"Here's what we think we're dealing with, folks," said Burwell. "According to our eyewitness, Kyle Simpson, there could be as many as three incendiary devices attached by triggering mechanisms to a door of a laboratory on the third floor."

Kyle Simpson?!

It was the first time Suzie had heard Kyle's name mentioned as the individual who had made the initial discovery of the threat. She beamed at Carrie, as though she was a cat who had just swallowed a canary.

Max turned to Carrie.

"Dr. Bloomfield, it would aid us immensely if you could describe to us the nature of the biological and chemical hazards we might encounter inside."

"Certainly," replied Carrie. She turned to the other agents.

"We have oxygen, nitrogen and flammable gas cylinders in almost every laboratory in the building. In addition, most of the labs contain liter bottles filled with strong acids and bases. There are also radioactive isotopes—both alpha and beta emitters. Most of the isotopes have a short half-life of decay. There is a wide variety of toxins in many of the labs. The central lab cluster—where the suspect devices were reported seen—contains Salmonella, Listeria, E. coli, and Clostridium. There is an inventory list of toxic and caustic materials next to the door of each lab. Under these circumstances, however, it would be extremely unwise to assume that *anything* inside the premises is currently located where it should be – or, for that matter, that it's properly contained."

"Excuse me, Doctor." The voice belonged to Special Agent Robert Foster of the FBI. "Clostridium? What is that, exactly?"

"In a nutshell, Special Agent Foster, Clostridium is an anaerobic bacterium that lives in tight, airless spaces. It makes a toxin called botulism. Botulism is a nerve toxin that is known to cause serious paralytic illness. In some cases it can be fatal. In our environment, it's stored in sealed containers in a special storage closet. But if it were in use in an on-going experiment, the Clostridium bottles might be situated under a fume hood. The bottom line is, you don't want to be exposed to it."

For Carrie, it ultimately came down to what made the most sense. Even though she had not been asked to do so, Carrie volunteered to lead a small team consisting of ATF, FBI, local fire department, and state police bomb squad personnel into the lab area. She and they suited up in the van. When they were finished, the group stepped out en masse into the bright sunshine wearing bulky, white bunny suits. Each person carried an additional eight kilograms of weight in the form of Kevlar body armor. Television crews zoomed in on the team as they walked toward the front of the building.

"You don't have to do this, Carrie," Max Burwell said.

"I know. But if someone *has* booby-trapped the lab, you'll need all the help you can get. Besides, Max, I'm not sure I could readily identify all of the toxins and other radioactive isotopes remotely via radio."

"Ready?" asked the ATF agent of the group members.

"Let's do this," replied one of the Massachusetts State Police bomb disposal experts.

The entourage of bunny-suited lawmen, led by Carrie Bloomfield, Ph.D. entered the front door of VBI.

To say that she felt some trepidation would have been a gross understatement.

CHAPTER FIFTEEN

The FBI was holding Chulbul Roy without bail at the Plymouth County Corrections Facility pending formal charges. He was cooperating fully with the authorities. Agent Sandra Mallory laid down her most recent report on Foster's desk.

"Roy was promised a hundred thousand dollars to lure Carrie Bloomfield to the equipment room in the early morning hours when the building would presumably be empty," said Mallory. "He faked an equipment malfunction that triggered a text alert to her phone. Roy was told by his contact that the release of the gas was only to intimidate Bloomfield into giving back secret research information she had stolen from a company. He told Roy that Bloomfield wouldn't be in any real danger, since Bloomfield could readily smell cyanide gas—therefore, she would never actually enter the room."

Mallory continued.

"Roy gave us the alias of the man: Forrester. Of course, there is no one on file with that name at the biotech company in question. Roy *was* able to give a reasonable description of his contact to the sketch artist. We're showing it to neighbors and to Whitehead employees today. Roy lives in a residential neighborhood, so we had no luck with ATM or other commercial security cameras. We're running the sketch through IAFIS along with the DNA sample."

Foster thumbed through the pages of her report. His eyes

stopped on one particular paragraph; he looked up.

"Oh, I see. 'Outside of Roy's apartment.' Says 'suspect discarded a cigarette butt.' Good."

"Roy says that his contact arranged for him to pick up the container of potassium cyanide at an abandoned warehouse on Marginal Street in Chelsea three days before the attack," continued Mallory. "We're looking at security camera footage from two ATMs nearby that face the warehouse. Perhaps we'll get lucky."

"Okay, good work, Sandy." Foster paused for a moment. "Say, what about the other lead—the headhunting outfit in Manhattan? The guy that called Bloomfield under the guise of offering her job?"

"Harris is checking that out. As your friend Jake Shapiro said, they seem to be a legitimate outfit. Several levels of shell companies lead to Furst AGW. It's not going to be easy to connect any dots between Premiere and Furst AGW—or whatever you want to call them—and the Whitehead attack, I'm afraid."

"Yeah, I think you're right," said Foster. "Tell Harris to keep working it, though. Thank you."

* * *

Dwight Stone sat in his luxurious sixteenth-floor corner office in the Furst Building in downtown Houston. As the Special Assistant to the Chief Operating Officer of Furst AGW, Stone was responsible for special projects—corporation shorthand for "black ops."

Stone's job was to keep the people above him happy. But at that moment, Stone himself was not happy. In fact, he was fuming over a confidential report he had just received that morning from the firm's corporate security officer in New York. Stone was finding it increasingly difficult to do his job, which was to keep people happy. It seemed that a potentially new and disruptive alternative energy technology was on the verge of slipping from the company's hands.

Stone picked up the phone and angrily stabbed at a button.

"Maggie, get me Jeff Howser in our Manhattan office."

* * *

"Jeff, what the hell's going on? You told me two weeks ago that we were making headway in the matter. And today, I'm reading your report. What's this 'domestic terrorism' bullshit? I told you to intimidate her, not to…eliminate anyone! Also, why is the FBI suddenly snooping around our Premiere office? What links do they have? There'd better not be any blow back."

"No, sir. Squeaky-clean. The, uh, *casualty* was unplanned, and most unfortunate. Our target brought along her boyfriend that morning. It was just shitty luck that he entered before she did."

Howser continued.

"The feds picked up the Indian kid, but he doesn't know squat. The only contact he had with us was through Sam Jenkins, one of our contractors. And Sam left this past Monday on a lengthy assignment in Dubai. He'll be out of pocket for at least six months."

"But you still haven't answered my question. What's the link back to us?"

"Unknown, sir. We're checking."

"Where are we on the surveillance?"

"We're running into some road blocks. Bloomfield's attorney's firm has placed protection on her around the clock. And a counter-surveillance crew, too. They're good. They've been sweeping both her apartment and the lab on a regular basis. They've cleaned us out twice now."

"Research materials? Patents? Anything?"

"Not yet. She keeps the important notes and lab books locked up in a safe in a secure part of the building. It's the same place where they lock up all of their dangerous chemicals and radioactive isotopes. We haven't found a way to get there unnoticed."

"The law firm?" asked Stone.

"As far as we can tell, both the firm and Bloomfield are using high-level encryption programs to send work product via email and to store backup copies to the law firm. We've been poking around their offices to see if they have any vulnerability. Unfortunately, they have excellent security. The servers are locked up tight. We're working the social engineering angles now."

"So," said Stone. "You're telling me that you've got squat. *Right?*"

There was a pause on the other end.

"I'm not gonna bullshit you, Mr. Stone. Yes, we're behind at the moment."

Stone paused a moment to rub his temples.

Finally, he said, "Okay. Listen—make her the offer based on the terms we discussed. Keep me in the loop. You've got my personal cell number. I *especially* want to know if the feds make any more inquiries at our Manhattan office—or at *any* of our other offices. Got it?"

* * *

Chulbul Roy was a 25-year-old postdoctoral fellow employed at the Whitehead Institute for Biomedical Research at M.I.T. Chulbul had received his doctorate in biochemistry from Princeton two years before. After a brief post-doc stint at Princeton, Chulbul felt it was time to move on. The position at M.I.T. seemed to be just the ticket.

Roy grew up in Guwahati, one of the largest cities in the Assam province in Northeast India. His family belonged to an upper caste and were well respected. They were also relatively wealthy. Chulbul had two brothers: one graduated with a doctorate in engineering from a university in the U.K.; the other was finishing up an undergraduate degree in philosophy at a prestigious school in The Netherlands.

As early as he could remember, Chulbul's parents instilled in him the belief that he must always strive to be successful and achieve great things during his life in order to bring honor upon the family name. Education, they reminded him, was the key to success. His father, Sunil, would sit patiently with his son for hours and tutor him in English. Sunil would tell Chulbul, "It matters not which path in life you choose. Just be sure that while you are on that path, you walk it straighter and faster and better than anyone else."

Although he tried telling himself that he was happy with his life,

Chulbul knew in his heart it was untrue. His mother and father had begun to pressure him lately to take a respectable bride. By that, they meant, 'find a bride from an upper caste.' In fact, they sent marketing materials to Chulbul from two companies—one in New York, and the other, in Washington, D.C.—which would, for a reasonable fee, arrange for women candidates from Assam province to join with him in the States.

Chulbul wasn't ready to settle down with a wife and a family. He was still trying to find meaning in his life. He loved his work in the lab. And he certainly had extracurricular interests like video games, and a multitude of friends from a MeetUp group consisting of Perl programming enthusiasts. Chulbul wanted to find a local cricket team or a gym to join. He was starting to get a little too pudgy around the middle. Joining a gym had been on his to-do list now for the past six months. He was reluctant to acknowledge that his BMI now put him squarely in the "obese" category.

At the rate I'm going, I will *have to participate in an arranged marriage if I am to ever have a woman someday. Now,* that *is certainly a depressing thought.*

Chulbul awoke from his dream. He rubbed his eyes and surveyed his present surroundings. He was sitting on a platform bed with metal springs. It held a thin, uncomfortable mattress, which, in turn, was covered by plain white bed sheets and a soiled woolen blanket. In one corner of his cell there was a short cabinet with two drawers that contained his change of clothes. Like his current clothing, the uniforms were of a drab olive color. Inscribed on the back of the prison garb were the words, "Property, Plymouth Co. HOC." Even his underwear bore the same stamp of ownership. In the other corner of his small world was a toilet. At one time, the toilet had had a seat cover. Chulbul guessed that a previous tenant had ripped it from its hinges. Near the toilet was a rudimentary sink and faucet. Above the sink was a scratched, but highly polished piece of metal bolted into the wall. The metal piece served in lieu of a bathroom mirror.

And now it's come to this.

Chulbul had allowed himself to be manipulated—to be used as a pawn in a ploy that had resulted in the death of an innocent man. Worse, he had brought shame to his family. He had dishonored his family's name.

Chulbul played out in his mind the events of the last eight weeks that led to his current nightmare.

The man had approached him one night at his apartment. He introduced himself as Jim Forrester. He said that he was head of security for one of the large biotech companies in the area. He flashed an ID badge at Chulbul and asked if he could come in.

Forrester had told him that his company had discovered one of its researchers had colluded with a scientist named Carrie Bloomfield, who worked part-time at the Whitehead. The two had smuggled out valuable proprietary materials: samples of an experimental compound, along with valuable data on its pharmaceutical properties. The company had spent millions of dollars on the new compound and was in the early stages of developing a promising new drug. According to Forrester, the company didn't yet have any evidence about a theft, so they couldn't expect any cooperation from the authorities. Forrester claimed to be laying the groundwork for an investigation.

"I can't go into a lot of details on this matter, except to say that she is also blackmailing a high-ranking employee at our firm. He's a good, honest, hard-working family man, and a close friend. Ultimately, we would like to obtain Dr. Bloomfield's cooperation, retrieve the stolen property, and keep this whole sordid matter out of the media, if possible."

Forrester went on to explain that Bloomfield wasn't taking the firm's polite requests to "resolve the matter to everyone's mutual satisfaction" seriously. Forrester proposed to enlist Roy's aid in a show of force that—according to Forrester—would not result in Bloomfield or anyone else getting hurt but, in his words, "would demonstrate in no uncertain terms to Bloomfield that we mean business."

Chulbul certainly knew of Carrie Bloomfield, along with her star reputation for being a brilliant researcher. It was rumored that the royalties on her patents had made Carrie Bloomfield a very wealthy woman. She was attractive and well liked. She could do no wrong. She had it all. Everyone adored her. Well, *almost* everyone.

Chulbul remembered thinking about her.

Living in a poor neighborhood in Cambridge. Riding her silly bicycle to and from the lab. Putting on such a false show of humility.

Chulbul had observed her interacting with the graduate students at the Institute. They hung on her every word. She seemed to care more for them than for Chulbul and his colleagues—he, and the more highly educated, mature postdoctoral fellows.

That's because we don't kiss her ass like the younger ones.

The information Forrester revealed had made perfect sense to Chulbul at the time. Bloomfield wasn't really the genius and miracle worker that everyone thought. She didn't deserve to be placed on a pedestal. In fact, she was nothing more than a common criminal.

What Forrester was proposing seemed dangerous. It was certainly illegal. Still, Forrester was offering him a lot of money in return for his assistance.

If no one got hurt…

If he didn't help, a well-respected company stood to be cheated out of hundreds of millions of dollars in revenue and years of valuable research because of her actions.

Forrester had promised Chulbul one hundred thousand dollars if he could help arrange for this *show of force*, as he called it. That amount of money was more than twice as much as Chulbul earned in an entire year! Chulbul didn't say yes to Forrester that night. But he didn't say no, either.

CHAPTER SIXTEEN

Carrie Bloomfield, along with the team of law enforcement officers entered the premises of Vital Biosphere, Inc. at approximately 10:25 a.m. After clearing the front door, they proceeded to the nearest stairwell and walked up to the third floor where the central core of laboratories was located. It was in this section that Kyle Simpson reported seeing several suspicious items sitting on a lab bench, connected to wires attached to a laboratory door.

The group approached one of three doors to the lab—the door Kyle said he used to safely enter and exit.

One of the bomb disposal members approached, and visually inspected the door and its handle for several minutes.

"Clear!" he shouted through the suit.

"Let me go first, Carrie," said Lieutenant Burwell to her.

"Nope. This is my lab. If anything is amiss, I would be the first to recognize it," she replied.

He nodded to her.

"Okay, everybody, listen up! Dr. Bloomfield will enter first. I want an orderly ingress, spaced out," shouted Burwell. "As you can see, it's difficult to be heard and understood while wearing these suits. So listen carefully, and watch for hand signals."

Burwell added, "Report *anything* that looks out of the ordinary: unusual wires, lights, any containers that are overturned or appear out of

151

place, et cetera. Let's go."

The bomb squad technician turned the door handle slowly, and he opened the door. Carrie went through first. Her field of vision was limited by the suit's helmet. She found it necessary to pan her head left-to-right to have a normal field of view.

Out of the corner of her helmet, approximately halfway down the closest lab bench to her left, she saw the devices that Kyle had described. Carrie started to take a step toward them. But something else caught her attention. *There*! It was a small amount of white powder under the edge of the table on the floor, next to the bench, tucked almost out of sight. The powder formed a tight, straight line approximately ten centimeters in length. She doubted that it was a spill; it looked as though someone had deliberately poured it. Alarmed, Carrie immediately held up her hand and made a fist.

"Freeze!" yelled Burwell to the others.

"What is it, Doctor?"

"Down there, Lieutenant. See it? Hand me a Geiger counter, please."

A state trooper reached through the doorframe and handed Carrie a small, portable counter.

Carrie turned it on. She bent down, and held the device a few inches from the powder. The meter immediately registered a loud clicking noise that could be heard by all present.

"It's okay. It's beta, it's not strong," shouted Carrie. "Probably Phosphorus-32 but I can't be certain."

Carrie explained to Burwell and the other team members that the radiation levels were not sufficiently strong enough to jeopardize anyone working in the room for short periods of time. They would need to wet the powder, covering it with towels, and then survey the area to determine the extent of the contamination.

She handed the counter to another member of the party, and proceeded down the hallway. Every few steps Carrie paused to survey her surroundings. She saw no other unusual containers or spilled substances that gave her cause for alarm.

Finally, Carrie reached the portion of the lab bench containing the devices. Other than a small, unmarked container half-filled with some sort of clear liquid everything appeared normal. She carefully avoided the wires, and put the mystery bottle in a sealed plastic bag, which she then handed to a team member standing behind her. Then Carrie motioned to the bomb disposal technicians to approach. She fell back to where Max Burwell was standing.

"Good work, Carrie," said the Lieutenant. "We'll need you to assist us again when we're ready to hit the next lab. But for now, go ahead and stand down while these guys go to work disarming this *thing*—whatever it is."

* * *

Four hours later, the team finished their inspection of the remaining labs, and Carrie exited the building and headed for the State Police mobile command center. There, she changed back into her street clothes.

Carrie exited the vehicle, half expecting to be accosted by television reporters. But instead, Suzie Beasley waited impatiently for her at the foot of the steps. Carrie would have welcomed the media instead.

"So, was Kyle *right*? Was it some kind of bomb?"

Just then, Lieutenant Burwell, who had been speaking to two police officers nearby, broke from the group and approached Carrie and Suzie.

"Doctor, come with us, please."

Suzie started to tag along behind the two. The Lieutenant noticed her. He stopped, and turned to Suzie.

"I'm sorry, Ms. Beasley. We need to speak to Dr. Bloomfield alone. Please excuse us."

Suzie looked like the little girl who had just been told she couldn't enter the boy's tree clubhouse.

Carrie and Max rejoined the group. One of the officers present was a Waltham police sergeant detective; the other, an ATF agent. The detective spoke.

"Carrie, the guy over there—Kyle Simpson—I think Max nailed

it from the get-go. The moment our boys arrived on-scene, Simpson was hell-bent on leading the charge inside to where he says he found the devices. We told Simpson we first had to wait for company management. Then we told him he wouldn't be allowed to go back inside. Well, Simpson got *real* upset and threw a hissy-fit when he heard that."

"Sounds like a classic hero to me," said Max.

"Oh, it gets even better," retorted the detective. "Simpson says he entered by the front door at around 7:15 a.m. That's true, according to the computer that logs all card swipes. The security camera in the lobby confirms it, too."

The detective sergeant turned to Carrie.

"You know about the back door, right? It's a conventional lock and key. No card reader. *But*... What our little friend over there didn't know was—the building landlord installed an additional security camera in the rear stairwell just last week."

"That's right," said Carrie. "We had to terminate an employee this past month. We suspected that he had a duplicate master key to the building. A few of our female employees were concerned for their safety. We requested that the management company install an extra camera."

"Well, *guess* who we saw on tape entering the back stairwell at 3:30 in the morning, only to leave approximately forty-five minutes later?"

The ATF agent spoke up.

"Yeah, and if you were wondering what was in the backpack he was seen wearing on 'candid camera'—well, let's just say that our boy's been doing a little on-line shopping these past few weeks. I just heard back from the other agents who entered his apartment armed with a search warrant. The history in his computer web browser shows that he's visited dozens of mail order web sites looking for places to buy electronic components; the same parts that went into that improvised device we disarmed upstairs. I guess Simpson won't be graduating to the ranks of master criminal any time soon. Not the brightest tool in the shed, huh?"

* * *

"Kyle Simpson, you're under arrest. You have the right to remain

154

silent. You have the right to an attorney. If you cannot afford one …"

Special Agent Foster read Simpson his rights as he led him away in handcuffs. Simpson's face had taken on an ashen appearance. Some of his fellow VBI employees were also in a state of shock. No one looked more surprised than Suzie Beasley.

A little later, Carrie overheard Jack Beasley say to his daughter, "I never did trust that little weasel! What in the *world* was he *thinking*? Was he really so warped as to believe he could pull off a stunt like this and get away with it?"

"I know what you mean, dad," replied Suzie. "I wanted Kyle terminated weeks ago. But certain people in R&D seemed to…"

Just then, Suzie looked over and saw that Carrie was standing within earshot and she was watching Suzie intently. The elder Beasley shot his daughter a puzzled look, wondering what she had intended to say. Suzie was clearly embarrassed. She did not utter another word.

Two days later, Carrie Bloomfield tendered her resignation at VBI. Jack Beasley was very unhappy. He couldn't understand Carrie's apparent sudden decision to leave the company. Beasley thought she was content in her role in heading up R&D at VBI. He held several private meetings with Carrie in an effort to learn the reasons behind her resignation. Ironically, the possibility of serious conflict between Carrie and his daughter, Suzie, had never entered the old man's mind. Carrie would tell him only that she was leaving the firm to "pursue new endeavors." She assured Jack Beasley that, although she had never signed a non-compete agreement, she would refrain from competing against VBI until the customary two-year period had elapsed.

Her parting words to Jack Beasley were: "It's been an honor to serve alongside you and to contribute to the growth of the company."

She had no parting words for the other Beasley.

CHAPTER SEVENTEEN

"Hey, buddy, why so glum?"

The fat, balding man placed his hand on Chulbul Roy's shoulder. Roy was sitting down at the picnic table in the prison courtyard. He was feeling absolutely miserable. Chulbul wanted to crawl into a hole and die.

Chulbul had been thinking a great deal about his life over the past seventy-two hours. His first year at Princeton had been full of wonders. It seemed as though there were no limits to what Chulbul could choose to engage in for enjoyment. The nightlife in Princeton, New Jersey beckoned – especially, the video game parlors. Chulbul had spent hundreds of dollars playing video games during his first semester alone.

During his second year as a graduate student, Chulbul, accompanied by several classmates, visited his first strip club. He was both repulsed and fascinated by the women who rubbed themselves against the metal poles and gyrated their bodies and bare bosoms in an effort to coerce money from the male onlookers. After a bit, Chulbul's friends decided that they would buy him a lap dance. He wasn't sure what a lap dance was, but he didn't want his friends to think he was a prude, so he accepted.

The blonde Caucasian girl they waved over was very shapely. She had a pretty face and petite breasts. She didn't appear to be much older than Chulbul. After a few seconds, she seemed to sense Chulbul's discomfort, and whispered into his ear, "Don't worry about your friends, honey. Just pretend they're not there. My name's Candy. What's yours? Is this your first time?"

She told him a second time to sit back and relax. It wasn't easy for Chulbul to do so. His friends, who were just a few feet away, were still teasing him. Chulbul recalled his embarrassment at getting an erection only a few short minutes after Candy started "grinding" in his lap. He was very aroused; she had nothing on except for a skimpy G-string. Finally, Chulbul leaned over and pleaded with Candy to get up from his lap. Chulbul was on the verge of panic; he was dangerously close to ejaculating in his pants. Candy obliged with a smile. She stood up and gave him a parting peck on the cheek. His friends cheered.

Chulbul returned to the present, and his current predicament. He finally registered the hand on his shoulder.

"Hey, pal. You okay?"

"Yes, thank you. I'm…I'm fine."

"Nice to meet ya', Fine. I'm Jed. Hey, if there's anything ya' need, just let me know. I've been in this hellhole now for almost ten years." Jed paused for a moment. He looked Chulbul up and down, as though he were sizing him up. "You're a handsome young man. You're new to the joint, right? So let me give you a word of friendly advice: you're gonna need some protection."

"Protection?" asked Chulbul.

"Yeah, you know—a friend. Someone with muscle. Like me, for instance. You see, some of these guys in here, they get a little hard up for companionship and they start gettin' ideas." He winked at Chulbul. "I'm sure you don't want that to happen."

Chulbul looked up at his newfound "friend" and felt even glummer.

* * *

"Take a look, and tell me your initial impressions."

Jake handed a document to Carrie. The two were enjoying coffee at an elegant table in the Conservatory Room at the Harvard Faculty Club. It was mid-afternoon; the two were the only patrons in the dining room.

Carrie quickly scanned the six-page fax. Her eyes paused on the last page. After a moment she handed the document back to Jake.

She frowned. "That's a lot of zeros."

"Yes, it is," said Jake. "This is how Furst AGW operates. They play rough and then, when they think you're scared, they try to buy you off with the big bucks." Jake chuckled. "With them, you get the good, the bad, *and* the ugly. I've seen it before."

Jake paused; his voice took on a more serious tone. "I'd be lying to you if I said this wasn't a lucrative offer."

Earlier that day, a law firm in Hartford, Connecticut, had sent the offer to Nexus Technologies in care of Jake's law office. The firm would not divulge the identity of their "client" but it didn't take any smarts to know that Furst AGW was behind it. In exchange for Carrie's current research findings, along with the transfer of ownership of all current and future provisional patents, intellectual property, and inventions, the "party who shall remain unidentified" would deposit $85 million cash into her account, along with a guaranteed lifetime royalty stream of one-half of one percent on all derived profits. Carrie would, of course, be required to continue working in a consulting capacity for a period of no less than 36 months, after which time the contractual arrangement could be extended for additional monetary compensation to be negotiated "at a later date."

Carrie shook her head: no.

"It's a lot of money, Jake. But, it was never about the money. Henry died trying to bring this technology to fruition. It belonged to him, and they murdered him to steal it. They murdered Paul and they tried to kill me."

Carrie stared down at her espresso. Her eyes narrowed.

"This has gone way beyond money. It's *personal*, now."

"I understand," said Jake. "It was my obligation to present you with the offer. I kinda figured what your response would be."

Carrie took another sip, and then she asked, "What are my options?"

"My advice? Drag this out for as long as possible. Their offer says five business days, but that's total B.S. I suggest that we send back a polite, stuffy response that says you're taking the matter under advisement, and that you'll get back to them no later than, say, twenty business days. Then, we follow up, asking for clarification on these sections *here, and here*, sequentially, of course. When they respond, we'll make counter offers." The last two sections Jake referred to described the disposition of related intellectual property, along with consulting requirements.

"We can probably drag this out easily for two to three more months without giving them any definite yea or nay. Who knows? By then, perhaps Robert's office will have made some headway in their investigation. In any event, it will give you more time for us to formulate a plan."

"That sounds good, Jake."

She took another sip, and added, coldly, "We need to find a way to screw these bastards."

Carrie seemed momentarily lost in her thoughts. When she returned, she said to Jake, "You know, I'd dump all of these specimens back into the ocean and burn my notebooks if it would bring Paul back again. You're pretty sure they have their hands on the same materials that Henry sent me—after they broke into his lab?"

"The police report wasn't meticulous in its detail, but our investigators spoke to Winship's postdoc. He said that only the containers from that last dive—along with his lab books—were among the items missing. So, yes, I'd say that it's a safe bet."

Jake motioned to the waiter for another round of coffee. After he and Carrie had been served, Jake said, "I see that you've been making some remarkable progress with the technology. Beth says there are at least three separate provisionals that we can carve out from the inventions you've made. And plenty of related stuff that we can use to box out any copy cats."

"Yes, the possibilities are enormous," she said. "I suppose I should be ecstatic right now. And I would be, were it not for the high personal price I've had to pay."

Jake nodded.

"I'll give this some of my best thinking, Carrie. Believe me, nothing would please me *more* than screwing Furst. They're the scum of the earth and I suppose, now, the sea as well."

* * *

Agent Sandra Mallory sat with Special Agent In Charge Robert Foster and five other agents of the Federal Bureau of Investigation in a conference room of their Boston headquarters at One Center Plaza. Mallory was briefing the other agents on their latest findings in the Whitehead Institute terrorism case.

"IAFIS in Washington came back with a hit on the DNA from the cigarette butt. It belongs to one Samuel E. Jenkins. Last known address is in Dallas, Texas."

"Priors?" asked one of the Special Agents seated at the table.

"No, not officially. Jenkins was an employee with Chesapeake Systems, a big defense contractor. If you recall, Chesapeake and Blackwater supplied much of the muscle for the State Department and many of the big companies doing reconstruction in Iraq and Afghanistan. Anyway, there was a shootout in the suburbs of Baghdad in '08 that killed nineteen civilians. Jenkins and three others were charged with manslaughter. They claimed self-defense. Seems that several key witnesses ended up disappearing prior to their trial, so the government had no choice but to drop its case against them."

"Jenkins renewed his license to carry in Virginia and Maryland last year. His credit card and bank accounts show him traveling and making withdrawals all over the country during the past twelve months. Boss, I know you'll definitely find this of interest: Jenkins' W4s link him to a subsidiary of Furst AGW called Secure Dynamics. They were paying him in the six-figures last year."

"Any recent transactions in Boston that would tie him to Dr. Roy?" asked Foster.

"No," replied Mallory. "But it's probable that Jenkins works under assumed names. We're checking the big three consumer credit databases looking for connections with other IDs."

"Good. This, along with a positive ID from Roy ought to be enough for a subpoena to go after Secure Dynamics' records."

Just then, the door to the conference room opened and a short, petite woman in her early sixties wearing "coke bottle" glasses handed a note to Foster. He took it from her and scanned it.

"Thanks, Jan."

Foster frowned.

"Damn. Well, lady and gentlemen, this is from the Superintendent of the Plymouth County Correctional Institute. It seems that Chulbul Roy was found dead in his cell this morning."

"How?" asked Mallory.

"Apparently another inmate slipped him a homemade shiv. He sliced his veins open and bled to death. Left a suicide note. They're checking the handwriting now to verify its authenticity."

Foster added, "In the meantime—Henshaw, Kelly: get hold of Dr. Bloomfield and see if she might be able to ID Jenkins from his photos. Perhaps he's been in close proximity to Bloomfield at some point. Circulate the photo around at the Whitehead, too."

"What about Secure Dynamics?" asked Mallory.

Foster thought for a moment.

"See if you can dig up an org chart on Furst AGW. I'd especially like to know who Secure Dynamics liaises with at corporate. Perhaps if we go high enough, we can rattle someone's cage, and cause them to show their hand."

"You want me to make some *indiscreet* inquiries, you mean?"

"That's *exactly* what I mean."

* * *

Jake Shapiro's stalling tactics with the Furst AGW's law firm continued. Five weeks had elapsed since the firm first communicated the offer to Dr. Bloomfield, but the two parties were deadlocked on item 5, paragraph 3, sub-section ii. And there were two disputed provisions in the contract to be addressed.

Ben Hathaway, the lawyer at the Hartford firm, represented

Gateway Enterprises. Unknown to Hathaway, Gateway was, in fact, a dummy corporation that sat several rungs down the ladder of dummy corporations under Furst AGW. Hathaway placed a call to Dwight Stone, a member of the board of directors of Gateway Enterprises and not coincidentally, an employee of Furst AGW in Houston, Texas.

"That's right, Mr. Stone. I'm getting the impression that the other party is not actually willing to come to the table. I've spoken by phone several times with Mr. Jacob Shapiro in Boston, the attorney representing Dr. Bloomfield. He's polite enough, and he says all the right things. But I'm pretty certain that he's stalling."

"You're certain that they're unwilling to compromise on the provisions that you've described?" asked Stone.

"I can't be a hundred percent sure," said Hathaway. "But if I were they, this is exactly what I would be doing if I wanted to stall."

Hathaway continued.

"Mr. Stone? If I may be so forward as to ask—is there anything else you'd like to tell me about this transaction? Perhaps it might aid me in the negotiations."

There was a pregnant pause on the line.

"No, there isn't, Mr. Hathaway. Please stand down and await further instructions for now. Thank you."

Stone hung up, and thought about his conversation with Hathaway for a moment.

Shapiro...Shapiro? Didn't we go up against him in court a few years ago? Yes, I remember that son of a bitch now!

Stone picked up his phone again.

"Maggie, get me Mr. Evans' office. See if you can schedule me in for a meeting later today or tomorrow. A half-hour tops. Thanks."

* * *

Special Agent In Charge Robert Foster was pleased with the pieces that were falling into place for the Whitehead investigation. Although they had suffered the loss of their key defendant-turned state's witness, Chulbul Roy, the DNA from a single discarded cigarette butt had allowed them to make a direct link to Furst AGW through Samuel E. Jenkins, an employee with Secure Dynamics. Jenkins came up in State Department records when his passport—rather, the passport belonging to his alias, Michael Matteson—was scanned when he had entered Dubai two months ago. His trip began exactly two days after the attack at the Whitehead. Foster assumed that his Secure Dynamics-Furst AGW handlers wanted him to be far away, in case anyone made a connection between him and his patsy, Chulbul Roy.

The Dubai authorities were currently detaining Jenkins a.k.a. Matteson, and Foster's team awaited his extradition back to the United States.

Foster decided that it was time to rattle the cage.

* * *

Dwight Stone was in his office, when the intercom beeped.

"Mr. Stone, there's a gentleman from the FBI—Special Agent In Charge Robert Foster—on line one."

Stone thought for a moment. There was little reason for him to try to duck the call. Stone had expected that one would come sooner or later. But he assumed it would be later—*much* later, in fact.

Best to get this out of the way.

Besides, he was scheduled to meet with Scott Evans, Special Assistant to the CEO, in one hour. It might be useful to find out what the Feds actually knew.

"Put him through, Maggie. Thank you."

"Hello, Special Agent Foster. Dwight Stone here. What can I do for you, today?"

"Hello, Mr. Stone. Actually, it's what I can do for *you*. This is a courtesy call. You see, you'll be interviewed in the very near future by a Special Agent from the Bureau in regards to your activities involving the terrorist attack at the Whitehead Institute at M.I.T. in Boston."

"Special Agent, I haven't the foggiest idea what…"

"Save it, Stone. See, here's what we know. Oh, and don't worry, you don't have to say anything right now. In fact, I wouldn't expect you to. Of course, I won't stop you from silently nodding in agreement should the mood strike you."

Foster continued.

"We know about Furst AGW's interest in the new technology that was being developed by the Woods Hole scientist, Dr. Henry Winship—now deceased. I could ask you what you know about Winship's death, and the burglary at his lab, but I don't want to get sidetracked just now. One murder at a time, I always say."

"So, Henry Winship sends the details of his discovery and the materials to a very smart researcher, Dr. Carrie Bloomfield in Cambridge, Massachusetts. Bloomfield works at the Whitehead, and at several other research labs. We also know that your goon, Samuel Jenkins, or, does he prefer to go by Michael Matteson? Anyway, Jenkins recruited a very willing and, might I add, extremely gullible accomplice by the name of Dr. Chulbul Roy, an insider who worked in the facility. Oh, did I mention? He's in prison right now, turning state's evidence. How am I doing so far, Mr. Stone?"

As Foster gleefully described the details of the case, Stone furiously scribbled notes to capture what the Bureau knew. Stone was horrified as to the amount and the quality of the information, but he kept his voice even and played along.

"This is all very entertaining, Special Agent. What will you do with this work of fiction? Perhaps you might enter next year's National Novel Writing Month competition?"

"I'll take that under advisement, Mr. Stone. But let me finish because I know that you're a very busy man and I don't want to keep you a moment longer than necessary."

Foster paused for a second, then he fanned a 100-page memo near the telephone microphone, hoping to give Stone the impression that he had volumes of material on the case.

"Just curious, now—let's see, where is it? Was it Jenkins' or Roy's idea to use the cyanide to intimidate Dr. Bloomfield? You know—the awful gas that killed Bloomfield's friend? Oh, here it is! I should have read this more closely before wasting your time with a needless question. I see that it was Mr. Jenkins' idea. Very clever! You see, *I* would have assumed that the *scientist* came up with that one."

Foster continued.

"We know that you weren't completely comfortable having your friend Jenkins anywhere convenient for us to question in the event we *did* make the connection to Furst. I understand. That was smart thinking on your part—sending him halfway around the world to Dubai. Unfortunately, it didn't quite work. The Dubai authorities have Jenkins in custody right now. He should be stateside shortly. Of course, we'll have Jenkins in protective custody for a little bit, so he might not have access to one of Furst's high-priced lawyers for several days. You know— Homeland Security. That should be plenty of time for him to decide whether to turn state's witness and corroborate much of this evidence."

"What do you want, Special Agent Foster?"

Foster thought Stone's voice betrayed annoyance.

Annoyance is good.

"As I said, Mr. Stone—nothing. This was merely a courtesy call. See, when our Special Agent comes calling, you'll not have to waste a lot of time rehashing all of this material. You *could*, however, be of tremendous assistance to us with respect to the Winship case. You see, we need just a *smidge* more facts and evidence to tie these two cases together. Since I'm uncertain whether you employed Jenkins for that particular job, it would sure be nice to know definitely. Did you, Mr. Stone? But, never mind—you don't have to answer that. I'm sure your attorney isn't present right now. But we'd love to reopen the case as a capital murder. It seems a shame to continue the charade that Winship died from an accidental drowning. Who knows? With a little bit of luck, we might even be able to tack on a conspiracy charge or two. Have a nice day."

* * *

Mr. Scott P. Evans, Special Assistant to the CEO, was furious with Dwight Stone. Their meeting started cordially enough. Evans had agreed to the briefing in order to find out where negotiations stood with Dr. Carrie Bloomfield, and her attorney, Jake Shapiro. Furst AGW had made a sizeable monetary offer to the woman scientist who, Stone believed, had made great strides in the research on the new, energy-generating life forms. Evans and his boss had every confidence that Stone would deliver on what could be a windfall for the company—conceivably, the biggest breakthrough in powering the planet since the discovery of fossil fuel. Evans, however, was not expecting to hear from Stone that the Federal Bureau of Investigation was breathing down their necks.

"Okay, Stone. Let me get this straight—one of our best contractors lets himself get caught by the Feds. They also captured that Indian doctor guy, *too*?"

"Yes. But Dr. Roy's getting caught was always part of the plan. He was set up to be the fall guy. And Roy never knew Jenkins' real identity. They must have found Jenkins some other way."

Evans got up and walked over to his wet bar. He poured himself a Scotch on the Rocks. He did not offer Stone a drink, however. Nor did he offer Stone a chair in which to sit. Stone remained standing; Evans sat down.

"This is some smelly piece of shit you're laying on me, Dwight. I tell you, if there's one thing the Old Man likes less than losing money, it's trouble with the law."

Evans took a gulp from his Scotch, and then he said, "Is there anything else I should know about?"

"No, sir. Just, the Agent In Charge of the Boston office indicated that I should expect to be questioned soon. I'll arrange for corporate counsel to be present, of course."

"Uh huh. Any idea how this got traced back to you, personally?"

"No, sir. I…" Stone started to speculate as to the answer, but then he thought better of it and decided to stop talking. "No."

"Tell me about the girl. Bloomfield? You say she's not going to budge?"

"According to the attorney representing our interests in the negotiations, his opinion is that she and her attorney are stalling and that they have no intention of completing a deal. I think he's right. I remember this guy, Shapiro. He gave us a pretty hard time in another case several years back. This may be personal for him."

"Personal? Ya' think?" asked Evans. "Ya' *think*?!" There was sarcasm in his voice.

"In fact, don't you think it might be a little *personal* for Bloomfield, too? After all, didn't her boyfriend end up being 'collateral damage?'"

"Yes. Yes, he did. I admit, it wasn't our best work, but…"

"Shut up, Stone."

Stone nodded slightly to Evans, and turned his eyes to the floor.

"The timing of this whole thing couldn't be worse. I had hoped that we would have closure on this in time for next month's stockholder's meeting."

Evans thought some more. After a moment, he resumed his questioning of Stone.

"How far have our industry scientists gotten with their specimens and that Woods Hole guy's—what's his name? Winfield?—with the stuff from his lab?"

Stone decided it best to not correct Evans on the scientist's name.

"Not very far, I'm afraid," replied Stone. "It's cutting edge science. There are perhaps only a few people in the world with the expertise to pull this off. Bloomfield is one of the best and the brightest."

Evans appeared to be speaking to himself now.

"If she's not going to play ball then ultimately she's of no value to us. And if we can't have her, then no one else will, either."

Then Evans said, "Stone, I understand that research laboratories can be dangerous places. Make it look like an accident. But for Christ sakes—use something other than cyanide this time."

"Can we get what we need from her work place? Lab books? Latest research? Preliminary patent information? Specimens?"

"I'm working on the final plan now. She keeps everything locked up pretty tight. It'll be difficult, but not impossible."

"Good, good."

Evans motioned with a flick of his wrist that their meeting was over. Stone turned and started to leave, but Evans had one final instruction for him.

"Stone?"

"Yes sir?"

"Don't fuck it up this time, okay?"

CHAPTER EIGHTEEN

"Let!" shouted Jake Shapiro to Robert Foster, his squash opponent.

"Are you sure about that?" replied Robert.

"Positive. Would I lie to an officer of the law?"

"I recall a certain incident in the basement of Langdell Hall in 1981 when the campus police ..."

"Yeah, yeah. Okay, you got me there. 'Let' it is, then. Shall we take a quick break?"

The two walked out of their court in the Hemenway Gym on the Harvard Law School campus, ducking to pass through the confines of the little door. They went to the vending machine and each selected a bottle of water, then they settled down on a bench nearby. Robert wiped the sweat off his bald head with a towel.

"How's our gal holding up?" asked Robert, referring to their mutual friend, Carrie Bloomfield.

"Okay, I think. The funeral in New Jersey was hard for Carrie, but she's gotten a lot of emotional support from her two close friends— Terrance and Edward. You've met them, right? At my party last year?"

"Yes. They're quite colorful. I think the older one was trying to hit on me."

They both laughed.

Robert took another swig from his water bottle, and then he said,

"Such a terrible tragedy—Paul Santiago."

Robert continued, "I shouldn't be telling you this, Jake, but I know you'll keep it confidential. We're making good headway in the Whitehead case."

"I'm glad to hear that, Robert. Carrie asked me yesterday if I'd heard anything from you. I know that you're not at liberty to discuss ongoing investigations, so I didn't want to pry."

"Well," replied Robert. "I had a chat a few days ago with a certain individual who is very high up on the food chain at Furst AGW. I wanted to try to rattle their cage a bit, to see what might fall out."

Robert continued.

"Remember the postdoc who unleashed the cyanide? Chulbul Roy?"

"Yes."

"Unfortunately, he committed suicide two weeks ago at Plymouth County Correctional. We're keeping it hush-hush for now. The good news is we've picked up the guy who was his handler. And we've established a direct link between him and one of the Furst AGW companies. He hasn't cracked yet under interrogation. But, surprisingly, he hasn't lawyered up either. I think he'll cooperate in exchange for a reduced sentence."

"That *is* good news, Robert. I'll obviously keep this between just the two of us."

"Jake—what I said earlier—about rattling the cage?"

"Yes?"

"Tell your guys who are keeping watch over Carrie to be extra vigilant. My call may have spooked the people at Furst into making a move on her."

"I understand. Thanks for letting me know."

Jake took one more swallow from his water bottle, emptying it. Then he said, "Now, are you ready to get back in there and let me kick your ass?"

CHAPTER NINETEEN

Carrie had just finished up a two-day experiment with the "worm juice" and was recording the results in her lab notebook when she heard a knock on the lab door.

"Dr. Bloomfield?" a woman asked.

"Yes."

Carrie looked up to see an attractive woman who appeared to be in her mid-40s. She sported eyeglasses with large lenses, an overabundance of lipstick and makeup, along with long brunette hair tied up in a bun.

"Hi, I'm Kelly Babcock. I'm a new postdoc in Dr. Bernstein's lab down the hall."

"Pleased to meet you, Kelly. As you probably know, I'm only a visiting staff scientist here at the Whitehead."

"Oh, please! It's an honor to meet you, Doctor. You're far too humble." She extended her hand to shake Carrie's.

"One second."

Carrie peeled off one of the latex gloves she was still wearing, and then she shook Babcock's hand.

"Everyone's told me about you, Dr. Bloomfield. I hear that you're brilliant! And, you're working on some really exciting stuff here."

"Please, call me Carrie. Yes, it does have some fascinating potential. I'm curious, though, who's been telling you about my work?"

173

"Oh, several people. I don't remember their names now. I'm terrible with names anyway, and this is only my second day here."

"I see," replied Carrie. "Well, welcome to the Whitehead. If there's anything I can do to help, please don't hesitate to ask."

Babcock paused for a second.

"I hope you don't mind my asking. Dr. Bernstein is out on vacation for the next few weeks. Well, I was wondering if I might hang out with you for a few days—just to get my feet wet. I promise I'll not be any trouble."

She smiled sweetly at Carrie.

Carrie thought for a moment. It might be nice to have an extra pair of hands for some of the experiments she'd be doing over the next few days. Yet, something about Kelly made Carrie feel suspicious.

Perhaps I'm being too judgmental because she's so patronizing. And she reminds me of a playboy bunny disguised as a scientist.

Carrie sighed. "Okay. You have a deal. I'll see you tomorrow around ten."

* * *

Kimberly Porter hailed from Missoula, Montana. An Army brat, she had grown up on military bases during her childhood. Her father was stationed at Fort Hood in Texas at the time that her parents filed for divorce; she was 13 years old. Kimberly and her mother moved off base into a small house in Killeen, Texas.

Kimberly attended ROTC at the University of Kentucky, majoring in biochemistry. Afterward, she was accepted into the Air Force Academy in Colorado Springs, Colorado. She excelled at the Academy, placing near the top of her class. She served two tours, including a stint with a military police unit, achieving the rank of Captain. Later she was recruited away from the Air Force by the Central Intelligence Agency. She officially held a military analyst position at one of the Agency's facilities in Maryland. But what Porter actually did—what the CIA trained her for extensively, and what she was quite talented at—

was completely different. Kimberly Porter was known in the trade as a "wet worker"—a skilled assassin. In 2009, she left the Agency and went to work in the private sector. She was currently in the employ of Secure Dynamics. One of her working aliases was Kelly Babcock.

* * *

"Doctor…I mean, Carrie? I'm sorry, but I'm a little rusty at this. Should I be using a 200 or 20 pipetmen for this procedure?"

"You're measuring 50 microliters, so you need the one marked 200."

Rusty is an understatement, thought Carrie.

Kelly Babcock explained to Carrie that she had completed her doctorate almost eight years earlier after which she had stayed out of the workplace to care for her ailing mother until her death in the spring. It didn't surprise Carrie to see someone like Kelly exhibiting such poor lab skills. Newly minted PhDs were often at the mercy of their thesis advisors when it came to learning basic lab skills. Add to that the fact that Kelly been out of circulation all that time.

"Actually, wait a second. I just want to check your pipetting skills first. *Here…*" Carrie poured some tap water into a beaker and asked the woman to pipette 50 microliters of liquid into a small tube.

Babcock performed the pipetting; it looked reasonably accurate. Carrie gave her the nod, and then she resumed what she had been doing at the other bench.

When Carrie walked away, Babcock secretly stole a glance over at Carrie's lab notebook on the desk. The notebook was half filled; its cover was labeled, *Nexus Technologies: Project Winship, book #6.* After disposing of Bloomfield, it would be important for Babcock to secure the other five notebooks, along with the original materials Winship had sent Bloomfield that were kept locked in the safe in the basement of the building. Babcock knew that Carrie's ID card, which she kept on a lanyard around her neck at all times, would open the door to the locked basement room. Babcock was reasonably certain from her CIA training that she could break into the safe. From intel gathered previously,

Babcock knew the safe was relatively low-tech in its design. All she needed was a good stethoscope and a reasonable amount of time to move the tumblers. Five to ten minutes would probably suffice.

* * *

Bob Sullivan sat in his late-model Ford outside the Whitehead Institute for Biomedical Research off Main Street in Cambridge, reading the *Boston Herald*. He was scanning the NFL scores after a full weekend of games. It appeared as though the Packers were headed for an undefeated season. The same could certainly not be said for Indianapolis. They had yet to win their first game this season. Payton Manning's neck injury had killed all hopes of the Colts having a decent year. And the Patriots would almost certainly wreak havoc upon them the next week in Foxboro.

Sullivan worked for Howe & Dodge Security. He enjoyed the work. The routine was much like that of a law enforcement officer—hours of complete and utter boredom, punctuated once in a blue moon by moments of sheer terror. Their biggest clients were law firms that wanted to get the lowdown on a philandering husband or a client who had been fraudulently sued for personal injury and who needed to catch the shyster in the act of doing something stupid, like going to the gym and lifting weights, or playing sixteen rounds of golf when they were supposed to be confined to bed or a wheelchair. These days, however, the law firm of Brack, Doyle and Peabody was paying Sullivan and five other private investigators handsomely to tail a professor by the name of Carrie Bloomfield. She had already been the target of a terrorist attack a few months earlier. Sullivan had been off-duty the morning that some whacko scientist unleashed a cloud of cyanide gas that almost took her out, and *did* take out her boyfriend.

Sullivan felt badly for the woman. She seemed like a nice person, not at all "hoity-toity" as you might expect from someone who had attended an Ivy League school. In fact, she was pretty "plain Jane." What surprised Sullivan was that she rode her bike or the MBTA everywhere she went.

It was nearly 9:00 p.m. His instructions were to call her on the hour and check in. If she failed to answer or did not return his call within ten minutes his instructions were to check with security at the front desk, and then go meet her in person. She was always very good about returning missed calls; consequently, he had only needed to hunt her down once in the past two weeks.

"Excuse me!"

Sullivan's thoughts were interrupted when a woman tapped on the passenger side window of his car. Sullivan rolled the window down a few inches. She was very attractive, sporting long, brunette hair. She was leaning over to speak with Sullivan. Sullivan couldn't help but notice her cleavage.

"I'm sorry to trouble you. I'm parked a half block down the street, and I think I'm having car problems. I opened the hood, and it looks like one of the wires that attaches to one of the *thing-a-ma-jiggies* may be loose. Could I trouble you to take a quick look at it?"

Sullivan looked at his watch. He still had six minutes until he needed to check in with Bloomfield.

"Sure."

Sullivan walked back with the woman and saw that she was driving a late model Toyota Camry. The hood was open. He pulled out a flashlight from his pocket and bent over to look more closely at the engine block.

"Which wire did you…"

Sullivan felt a stabbing pain, just above his elbow. He looked up and saw a needle protruding from his arm. Then the lights went out.

* * *

Carrie was loading up the last of the test tubes in a Styrofoam container that held liquid nitrogen. She would transport the tubes to a special cylinder located in another part of the building that was designed to keep the samples at a constant 72 degrees Kelvin. These samples would be thawed for use in later experiments.

"Oh, hello, Carrie! You're still here. Good!"

177

Carrie looked up to see the new postdoc, Kelly Babcock, standing in the doorway. Babcock seemed nice enough, but Carrie was glad she didn't have to work all the time with Kelly. The woman talked incessantly. When Carrie first met the woman, her "radar" told her that there was something a bit off about Kelly. Carrie knew that she shouldn't dislike Kelly, but the woman reminded her far too much of Suzie Beasley, the CEO's daughter at Vital Biosphere.

"Yes, but I'm leaving very soon. I just need to make one final entry in my notebook."

"Oh, okay," said Kelly. "I wanted to ask you something. It's not work related. Would you have a minute to chat after you're finished?"

Carrie suppressed the urge to sigh.

"Sure. Just give me a moment. Please, sit down."

Kelly sat down at the desk on the opposite side of the aisle from Carrie. It was situated behind Carrie, slightly closer to the door, near the sink. Carrie picked up her pen to resume writing.

That's odd.

Carrie noticed that it was 9:02 p.m. She had expected a call from Bob Sullivan by now. Bob was on duty, and stationed outside in his car. She made a mental note to call him in a few minutes. Best to do it before she got tied down in a long chat with Kelly. Carrie didn't want Bob to fret or to come in the building looking for her as he had last week, when Carrie had accidentally left her phone in the ladies' room.

Carrie continued transcribing a series of numbers from a scratch piece of paper into her notebook. She happened to catch movement out of the corner of her eye; it was a reflection of Kelly from the glass door of the cold box.

WHAT THE…!!

Kelly was standing with her back turned to Carrie. But the reflection showed Kelly drawing liquid into a syringe from a small bottle, and then tapping the side of it to clear the syringe of any air bubbles. Kelly then put her hand holding the syringe back into her lab coat pocket. Without saying a word, she started to walk slowly toward Carrie.

Carrie tried to remain calm. She kept writing with her right hand, while with her left, Carrie slowly reached out to the Styrofoam container and lifted the lid off.

Just as she got behind Carrie, Kelly lifted the needle and aimed for Carrie's neck. But Carrie was a split second faster; she immediately flung the lidless Styrofoam container up and behind her, toward Kelly's head. Liquid nitrogen and test tubes flew up and hit Kelly squarely in the face.

"AAAAAHHHHHHH!!!"

Kelly was momentarily blinded from the liquid. She flung her arm wildly in front of her, hoping to catch—and stab—Carrie with the needle. One swing narrowly missed striking Carrie in the hand.

Carrie ducked and escaped around Kelly. Kelly followed a moment later, in hot pursuit. Unfortunately, Carrie left her cell phone sitting on the lab table.

Running quickly, Carrie rounded a corner and headed toward the stairwell. But Kelly had anticipated Carrie's actions; she had gone in the opposite direction and reached the stairwell ahead of Carrie. Carrie retreated.

Babcock was in excruciating pain from the cold burns on her face caused by the liquid nitrogen at minus 321 degrees Fahrenheit. Some of the liquid had splashed into a corner of Babcock's left eye, leaving her vision blurry. It had also singed her eyebrow, as well as the entire left side of her cheek and jaw. Bloomfield's defensive action had been entirely unexpected. She was furious with herself for not suspecting something was amiss when the scientist had casually reached over to pick up the container lid.

She heard a door shut down the hallway.

There!

Ahead of her, lying on the floor outside of a room was the lanyard containing all of Carrie Bloomfield's ID cards! She had to be inside.

I'd better get in there quick, before she finds a phone and calls the police!

Babcock raced up to a door. The sign on the door read, "Anaerobic Culture Facility." She listened for a few seconds. She could hear no talking or indications of movement inside.

Careful! Make sure she's not hiding behind the door. This could be a trap.

Babcock tried the door, but it was locked. Then she recalled that she had Bloomfield's lanyard. Babcock searched through all of the ID cards until she found the one that was labeled "Whitehead Institute." She swiped it against the reader, and was rewarded with a loud "click." Babcock pocketed the lanyard in her lab coat and then she retrieved a wicked-looking military switchblade from her back pocket. She flicked it open.

* * *

The assassin carefully opened the door. Inside was a hatch that appeared to be connected to some sort of air lock. Just then she heard another door in front of her close.

Bloomfield has to be directly ahead, on the other side!

Babcock unlatched the door, and raced inside. It was a small room, barely large enough to accommodate a single person. The room had another door opening into a larger, second room. This door had a porthole. Babcock could see Carrie Bloomfield ahead, standing inside a slightly larger room, next to another door. Bloomfield looked up, and saw her pursuer. There was a loud click; Babcock saw Bloomfield open yet another door and scamper inside to the next compartment. Babcock gave chase.

The pursuer had to wait for the light on the door to turn from red to green; finally, Babcock got the door opened and went inside. She could see that Bloomfield was standing on the opposite side of the door, in front of the porthole, looking at her. The two stood eye to eye. Bloomfield watched her intently. Babcock attempted to open the latch, but the light indicated red. Babcock stabbed at the button. Nothing was happening.

Babcock was feeling fatigued from the chase—possibly going into shock from the cold burns.

Bloomfield must have locked this door somehow.

Something was wrong with this picture. She needed to stop and think for a second. She needed to clear her head.

Why would Bloomfield barricade herself in this tiny, enclosed roo…

Like an old-fashioned television turning off, Babcock was suddenly aware that her field of vision had contracted into a small circle. She was also cognizant of a loud buzzing noise in her ears. She felt as though she was intoxicated. Then, it dawned on her what Bloomfield had done! Babcock turned around and started for the door behind her, but a second later she collapsed onto the floor, unconscious.

* * *

"Catherine, we're live in…FIVE…FOUR…THREE…"

The cameraman silently mouthed the words TWO and ONE, and then he pointed to the television news reporter.

Tom, we're here live in front of the Whitehead Institute for Biomedical Research on the M.I.T. campus where, less than an hour ago, police responded to a report of an attempted assault against one of the researchers who works here, Dr. Carrie Bloomfield. We spoke a moment ago with an Institute security guard. He explained that a woman whom police have identified as forty-four-year old Kelly Babcock of Quincy came after Bloomfield with a hypodermic needle filled with an unknown substance—and also, a switchblade knife. Bloomfield fought off Babcock by throwing a container filled with extremely cold liquid nitrogen at her, causing third-degree cold burns to the left side of Babcock's face.

Tom, this is where things get even more bizarre—Babcock pursued Bloomfield into what's known as an Anaerobic Culture Facility room in this building. According to the guard, Bloomfield actually tricked Babcock into standing for several minutes inside a room containing a pure nitrogen atmosphere, where scientists keep bacteria that can live only in the absence of oxygen. Bloomfield was somehow able to outlast her alleged attacker in this room. Once Babcock was incapacitated, Bloomfield disarmed her of a military-style switchblade, and restrained her using plastic tie-wraps.

Bloomfield then activated an emergency system to flood the room with oxygen, which triggered an alarm at the main desk—in turn, alerting the security guard. Bloomfield reportedly performed mouth-to-mouth resuscitation on her alleged attacker. An eyewitness on the scene says in so doing, she probably saved Babcock's life. EMTs here at the scene are working on Babcock at this moment.

Tom, our viewers may recall that Eyewitness News reported on another attack right here at the Whitehead Institute three months ago involving Bloomfield. FBI agents arrested another Whitehead researcher, Chulbul Roy, of Cambridge, for allegedly unleashing a cloud of poisonous cyanide gas in the early morning hours of November 29th. Bloomfield was his apparent target. She narrowly escaped, but a companion, twenty-seven-year-old Paul Santiago of Somerville, succumbed to the gas and was pronounced dead on arrival at Massachusetts General Hospital. Roy is currently being held without bail on domestic terrorism charges in the Plymouth County Correctional Institute.

Catherine, have police speculated as to the reason behind the alleged attack on Bloomfield by Babcock? And are they drawing any connection between the earlier cyanide attack and tonight's attempted assault?

Tom, police say it's too early to speculate as to the motive behind tonight's attack, so we'll just have to wait and see what develops.

Just then, the reporter was handed a note from someone off camera. She paused for a second to read it, and then she began to extemporaneously deliver the remainder of her report.

Tom, there's been a new, late-breaking development in this story. I'm being told that Cambridge police have found a man locked inside the trunk of an automobile one block away from this facility. He's been identified as fifty-year-old Robert Sullivan of Revere. Sullivan is employed as a private investigator. Police believe that Sullivan was part of the protection team hired to guard Bloomfield in the wake of the earlier cyanide attack. Sullivan stated that a female attacker using a hypodermic needle drugged him.

Upon gaining consciousness, Sullivan kicked at the trunk lid until he was heard by a passing pedestrian.

Reporting live for Channel Seven Eyewitness News, this is Catherine Hayward, at the M.I.T. Whitehead Institute for Biomedical Research in Cambridge.

* * *

"So, it's the good Doctor Bloomberg. We meet again."

Detective Sergeant John Hatherley of the Cambridge Police Department faced Carrie in the lobby of the Whitehead Institute. A half-hour had passed since the alarm in the Anaerobic Culture Faculty had alerted the security guard in the building to trouble. The guard had called the M.I.T. Police. After that, all hell broke loose. Hatherley, and a dozen or so other law enforcement officers soon arrived. Cambridge Police had found Bob Sullivan, confused and weak but otherwise okay, locked in the trunk of his car on Main Street. The M.I.T. Police arrested Kelly Babcock. Two EMTs placed her on a gurney in handcuffs. They dressed her wounds and were checking her vital signs. She appeared to be lucid and responsive.

"Actually, Detective Sergeant, it's *Bloomfield*. Carrie Bloomfield. Would you like me to explain to you again how a machine can call a cell phone?"

"I don't think that'll be necessary, Bloomfield. It seems that you've managed to get yourself into trouble this time *without* the help of a multi-million dollar machine."

He pulled out a notepad from his back pocket and flipped to a blank page.

"Just so I understand it correctly—that broad over there—" he pointed to Babcock. "Kelly Babcock, is it? She was tryin' to kill you, but you got the drop on her first. Now, why daya suppose she'd wanted to do you bodily harm?"

"Gosh, I'm afraid she didn't take the time to explain to me her reasons for coming at me with a syringe filled with god-knows-what and a switchblade. Perhaps you could tell *me*. After all, *you're* the detective."

Hatherley sighed with disgust.

"What's your relationship with the accused?"

On a whim, Carrie replied, "We're lovers."

Hatherley shot Carrie a dirty look. She smiled back.

"She approached me asking for help with coming up to speed in the lab," answered Carrie, truthfully this time.

"I've been mentoring her for the past three days. But if I had to make an educated guess—but keep in mind, I'm not a detective—based on her lack of lab skills, she's probably not a postdoc at all but instead, someone who was contracted to kidnap or kill me."

"Oh, I see. Like in those *007* movies? Or *Mission Impossible*?"

"Yes. *Now* you're deducing!"

This time it was Hatherley's turn to feel exasperated. He slammed his notebook shut, and said loudly to Carrie, "This is *bullshit*, Bloomfield! If there's something you're not telling me, by God I'm gonna…"

A male voice interrupted.

"You're going to *what*?!"

The detective turned around, startled. Carrie thought Hatherley was going to jump out of his skin. Standing right behind him was Special Agent in Charge Robert Foster.

"Jesus! What *is* it with you sneaking up on me like that, G-man? You got a hard-on for this campus or what?"

"Hatherley?"

"What?!"

"Get the fuck out of here. NOW!"

* * *

Carrie Bloomfield sat with Jake Shapiro and three other attorneys of Brack, Doyle and Peabody in the firm's eighth floor conference room on State Street in downtown Boston. The object of their attention was a speakerphone placed in the middle of the table. Ben Hathaway, the lawyer at the Hartford, Connecticut, firm representing Gateway Enterprises was on the other end. Joining Hathaway from

Houston, Texas, was his client, Dwight Stone.

After a round of introductions, Jake was the first to speak.

"Mr. Hathaway, Mr. Stone, let's cut to the chase, shall we?"

"Agreed," Stone and Hathaway both replied.

"For the sake of argument—and so we don't drive one another crazy with company names and entities—let's just refer to *your* side, Gateway, Rockland, Secure Dynamics, Premiere, et cetera, as 'Furst AGW' and *our* side as 'Dr. Carrie Bloomfield.' Okay?"

There was a slight pause. Stone answered, finally.

"Sure. But you've made it abundantly clear that Bloomfield is not interested in negotiating any kind of a deal with Gate-…with Furst AGW. So, what do you want?"

"Well, for starters," said Jake, "an apology for the death of Paul Santiago would be nice, followed by a second apology for the attempted murder of Dr. Bloomfield last week. But I know that's not going to happen today."

There was only silence from the other end.

Jake continued.

"Mister Stone, after you hear what we have to say today, it is my hope that Furst AGW will see the futility in mounting any further aggression against Carrie Bloomfield. In short, it's time to call off the dogs."

"I'm listening," replied Stone.

"Good. Tomorrow morning at the start of business, several trade journals that cover the alternative energy markets will receive a press statement from this office. The statement will summarize the most recent research findings by Dr. Bloomfield. Dr. Bloomfield will publicly announce that she's surrendering all claims on the technology, as well as existing provisional patents that our firm has filed on her behalf and assigning them to another party."

There was stunned silence on the other end.

"So what are you saying, Shapiro? That Bloomfield is handing over the goods?"

"No. You see, Mr. Stone, Carrie Bloomfield intends to ensure that all of it—the cell lines, intellectual property, and trade secrets remain *in the public domain.* They will be guarded under a very unique licensing agreement that we're currently working on."

Jake continued.

"You've heard of public domain software, haven't you, Mr. Stone? Well, if you're unfamiliar with it, I suggest you look up Richard Stallman and the General Public License on Wikipedia. You see, we're setting up an analogous model to it, and establishing a new corporate entity: a non-profit to be known as the Winship Foundation. It will provide material and resources, along with a pooled database to member companies and organizations that have a vested interest in developing this new alternative energy technology derived from the work of Bloomfield and the late Dr. Winship. That *can* include Rockland Global Energy and Furst AGW, if you join. But so, too, can your competitors."

Silence.

"Are you still there, Mr. Stone?"

"Yes."

Stone cleared his throat.

"Just how do you intend to make *your* profit?"

Carrie spoke up.

"I'm not sure you're grasping the big picture here, Mr. Stone. There *will be* no profits for the Winship Foundation or for me. Every member organization will start out on an equal playing field. You will all make money, but you will also be required to share your research data and findings."

Carrie continued.

"Think back to your days in kindergarten, Stone. Remember when you played in the sandbox, and you shared your toy with the other little boy? Well, our rules say that you *will* share, or you'll get *nothing*. The Winship Foundation will police the sandbox and watch over you."

"Why—why are you doing this?"

"It's very simple, Mr. Stone," replied Jake. "And elegant, too. I wish that I could take the credit for it, but it was Dr. Bloomfield's idea. If we level the playing field with this new non-profit and its public domain licensing structure, the world will benefit. And you and Furst AGW will have *far* less incentive to go around breaking into labs, stealing research notebooks, and killing people."

Stone was quiet. He was still trying to grasp the implications of this end-around that Bloomfield and her attorney had engineered.

His thoughts were interrupted when Bloomfield's voice came over the phone again:

"Do you wanna play in the sandbox or not, Mr. Stone?"

CHAPTER TWENTY

In the weeks that followed the attack on Carrie at the Whitehead, federal prosecutors unsealed an indictment against Furst AGW naming two high ranking employees of the company, Scott P. Evans and Dwight Stone, as co-conspirators under Chapter 96 of Title 18 of the US Code, commonly known as the RICO Act. Charges against Evans and Stone were eventually expanded to include capital murder in the death of Dr. Henry Winship.

Samuel E. Jenkins and Kimberly Porter, of Secure Dynamics, both refused free legal counsel from Furst AGW and instead decided to turn state's witnesses in exchange for a plea on lesser charges. All four individuals were being held without bail in the Federal Correctional Facility in Danbury, Connecticut. Their trials were scheduled to begin in two months.

The International Institute for Species Exploration announced a new species known as the Great Bioluminescent Winship Tubular Worm. Most scientists referred to it simply as "The Winship Worm."

A month earlier, the Winship Foundation Executive Committee had voted to delay consideration of the membership of Rockland Global Energy/Furst AGW. The committee reported that it would reevaluate Rockland's application after the ongoing legal case against its employees was settled.

Two companies in the Winship consortium were just a few

months away from releasing their first commercial products. One of the products would be incorporated into a state of the art solar farm under construction near Albuquerque, New Mexico.

Edward and Terrance's dog, Fee-fee, passed away from cancer. Carrie made a sizeable donation to the Angell Memorial Animal Hospital and Shelter in Fee-fee's memory. Terrance and Edward asked their friends to help commemorate Fee-fee's life with a private ceremony and burial. Edward had shoveled the better part of a morning, digging a hole approximately two feet by two feet by four feet deep. Terrance and Edward took turns giving moving eulogies for their beloved pet. There wasn't a dry eye among the group. Edward gently placed Fee-fee's remains, wrapped in a colorful cloth blanket, into the ground. Each person then took turns tossing a handful of dirt into the grave.

Fourteen months after Paul Santiago's death, Carrie went on a couple of dates set up by Terrance. The men were nice enough, and she truly enjoyed her time with them. But at the end of their evenings, Carrie found herself wanting something more. She tried telling herself that it wasn't fair to compare her suitors with Paul. After all, everyone was different—each man had his strong points and endearing qualities. But some small spark in the interaction was missing that distinguished "friend" from "future lover." Carrie hoped she would find that spark again someday.

* * *

"Carrie, to what do I owe the pleasure?"

"Hey, Jake. As you probably know, I've been conducting some interesting research with the Winship Worm, completely outside of the energy arena."

"Yes, the folks mentioned something about it at our staff meeting last week. You're working in the area of apoptosis, right?"

"That's correct. It seems that the worms' cells are unusually long-lived. They apparently lack the compound that signals the cell to die. Understanding this abnormal regulation will be an important tool in developing new cancer therapies and screening new anti-cancer compounds."

Jake chuckled.

"Judging by the excitement in your voice, may I assume you're on the cusp of some exciting new discovery that we can patent for you, Doctor?"

"I'm transferring the files over to you even as we speak. Jake. Hey, have I ever…"

"I know. You're going to ask, 'Have I ever told you that you're my favorite karky fixer,' right?"

"Well…no."

"No?"

"No. Although you *are*, of course."

Carrie continued.

"What I was *going* to ask before I was so rudely interrupted was—have I ever asked if you'd go on a date with me sometime? Perhaps come to my place for dinner on Saturday?"

There was silence. Carrie had no idea whether the stuffy attorney on the other end of the phone line was grinning from ear to ear, or if he was too stunned to reply.

"Don't keep me in suspense, Jake!"

"What kind of wine should I bring?"

Carrie could hear him smiling over the phone.

THE END

ACKNOWLEDGMENTS

Thank you to my friends who read this book when it was still but a manuscript. You provided me with thoughtful and valuable feedback: Susan Cassidy, Leslie Douglas, Eliot Mayer, Gail Page, Ken Porter, Bob Rowlands, Carole Roberts, Rick Sanger, and Robin Stratton to name a few.

To my loving spouse, Barb Ariel Cohen, Ph.D. you gave me your support and scientific expertise that led to a more accurate and believable narrative.

To my editors: Bettina Eliot, and Carole Groepl, you helped to polish this rough stone into a gem of fiction of which I could be proud.

To my publisher, Blue Mustang Press: you took a chance on a beginner novelist and made my dream come true.

Finally, to Michael C. Keith, Ph.D., a good friend and fellow writer: without your encouragement and mentoring, this novel would not have seen the light of day.

Any errors or omissions are mine alone.

www.ingramcontent.com/pod-product-compliance
Lightning Source LLC
Chambersburg PA
CBHW070828180626
46818CB00001B/436